Fruit Loops
the Serial
Killer

To Mary Lynn + Vic,
what a pleasure it has been to
become friends with you! I
forsee a long friendship!
Hope you enjoy! Keep on
bookin!

love,
Mary M Maurice

Fruit Loops the Serial Killer

By

Mary Maurice

HOLLISTON, MASSACHUSETTS

FRUIT LOOPS THE SERIAL KILLER
Copyright © 2016 by Mary Maurice

Cover Art by Joel Nakamura.

First printing September 2016
10 9 8 7 6 5 4 3 2 1

ISBN # 1-60975-173-6
ISBN-13 # 978-1-60975-173-9
LCCN # 2016946750

Silver Leaf Books, LLC
P.O. Box 6460
Holliston, MA 01746
+1-888-823-6450

Visit our web site at www.SilverLeafBooks.com

To Mom and Dad, Thank you.

Fruit Loops the Serial Killer

1

"My sweet lord, just wait a minute!" Candy Jane mutters under her breath as she scans the dining room, hoping no customers over-heard her ranting. Storming into the kitchen, she throws the half filled plates into the plastic bus tub, as Jose, the dishwasher, jumps away from the raging waitress and flying food.

"I'm sorry, Jose. Sometimes these people really get to me." She hisses through clenched teeth.

"Si Candeee. No problemo."

❊   ❊   ❊

Knowing he barely understands a word she's saying, Candy laughs, and pats him on the back, slyly removing a piece of chicken skin from his shoulder. "Later, amigo."

"Adios, amiga," he replies.

Heading back out to the front of the restaurant, Candy feels her good mood dissolve little by little, as once again, the night crew is late.

"They're never on time." Her brain screams in agony.

"Cane, hey Cane." A surely voice rises over the clatter of dishes, breaking Candy's thoughts.

Turning around, she sees Hector Toth stampeding toward her. "Oh, hell," she mumbles.

Dashing behind a table, Candy pretends to be wiping and arranging the condiments. Toth stops right in front of her; annoyed at being ignored. "When I call, I expect you to answer me. Do you understand?" His voice rising like an impudent child.

"I'm not in the mood for your anger, Hector. I didn't hear you." Sliding past him. "What do you want?"

Candy knows one of Toth's pet peeve's is being talked back too, especially by a woman.

Snarling. "I need you to stay and work the dinner shift, Melvin's sick, and there's no one else to fill in."

"What! No way, I've been in this hole all day, and I'm tired. Find somebody else!"

"There *is* nobody else." Toth's jaws grind. "I'll try to get you out of here early, there's nothing more I can do."

Candy Jane glances at the Swiss Miss figurine above the door. The hands angled toward five.

"I can't do it Toth, I've already made plans, and I'm not going to break 'em."

"With who, your dork boyfriend, Billy?"

Candy gawks at Hector Toth. "What, are you six?"

"You're staying, and that's final. I've discussed it with Sven, and he agrees."

"You called Sven?" Candy turns away whispering, "Jerk."

"What'd you say?" Toth inches closer. "You'd better be careful, missy. You think you've got it made here, well you don't. You watch, one day Sven is going to wake up to your antics and get rid of you."

"Yeah, okay Toth, whatever you say. Just remember, Sven already knows about my *antics*, and he likes them. Plus, you're not my boss."

"Well, tonight I am, and if you don't do this, then forget about coming in tomorrow."

"What are you saying?"

"I think I'm making myself pretty clear." She watches as his face reddens and his upper-lip begins to quiver. "Just do it." He spits, whipping around.

"Hey Candy Jane, my Christmas candy cane!"

The hairs on the back of Candy's neck stand on end as she hears Billy's voice. Time and again she's asked him not to call her by that nickname, but thinking it's cute, he continues to tease her.

Flicking around, she eyes him strolling toward her. Pretending not see Toth, Billy sidles up to Candy, planting a wet, beer smelling kiss on her cheek.

"Hey, Honey," he belches while sneering at Hector. "Toth, you're looking as ugly as ever. Your mom should've shot you when you were born, put you, and us, out of our misery."

"Shut up, Billy." Pushing him away.

Studying the grungy, thirty-one year old man whom she had been sleeping with for the past three years, Candy wonders where the attraction is. There has never been any real passion, and very little romance. The relationships is a casual one, which is fine with her.

Lately though, Billy's been hinting that he wants more. No way, even now the thought of hanging out with him is appalling.

"Okay, Toth, I'll work." Candy Jane announces, noticing Billy cringe.

"What do you mean, you're staying?" Billy whines. "We have plans."

"Hector needs me to cover a shift tonight. One of the guys called in sick."

"That's bullshit."

Glaring at Toth, who is submerged in their conversation, Candy barks. "Is there something else I can help you with, Hector?"

Turning on his toes, he marches into the kitchen.

"Loser." Candy snorts.

Squaring up to Candy Jane, Billy nuzzles against her. Pushing him away, she steps back. "What do you think you're doing?"

Flustered, she combs her hands through her hair, and scampering behind the counter, grabs a mini box of Fruit Loops. Ripping the top off, Candy pours the color coated cereal directly into her mouth.

"I can't believe you! Don't you realize we're in a public

place, a public place that's my job?" Dumping more morsels into her mouth. "Are you trying to get me terminated?"

"There you go again with that fancy college talk. Can't you just use normal words?"

"I only went to St. Cloud Community College for a year, Billy, and all I did was party."

"Yeah, but um, still." Stuttering.

"You're drunk." Candy moves out from behind the counter, as Billy rears.

"I'm not drunk. I only had a couple." He continues back peddling.

"I thought you weren't going to drink, Billy?"

"Are you going to start raggin' on me because I had a few beers? You're not my wife, or my mother."

"Thank my stars for that, I wouldn't want to be either one those poor women. What a cross to bear." Candy smiles, trying to break the tension.

Shyly, Billy moves closer to Candy. "Don't you get a little break before you have to start?"

"This is it." Hurling him away again. "Why are you being so needy?"

"I'm aching for some loving, babe."

"Listen Billy, I think the best thing you can do right now, is leave, go somewhere and sober up. Then maybe we can talk when I get off. I'm not doing anything with you if you're still wasted. Got that?"

"Candy, I'm not drunk. I'm just intoxicated with the idea of being with you."

"*Shut up!*" Candy says softly, stepping up to Billy and

kissing him on the mouth. "Why don't you go take a nap, maybe a shower, and we'll see what happens later, okay?"

Billy cants up to Candy Jane. She stops him with her outstretched arms. "You heard what I said, and I'm not joking."

"Okay, all right, I got it. Why don't you give me one more little kiss before I go? It's cold out there, and I need something to warm my blood."

"I'm sure there's plenty of booze in those veins keeping that blood warm."

"Real funny, Candy Jane." Feeling dejected, Billy peck kisses her on the cheek, and slinks toward the revolving door. "I'll be back at around eight."

"I'm not making any promises."

"Ah, how can you resist this?" Rolling his hips like Elvis.

"Yeah, right, how could I say no to *that*?" Waving as he wheels out, Candy Jane listens to the vacuum sucking sound of the revolving door as it whirls around.

Sighing, Candy lumbers over to the bus station to set up for dinner. She's not feeling well, but figures being here is better than hanging with Billy. She has to break it off with him; it's getting to be too much. Plus, he's drinking a lot, again.

Grabbing the coffee pot from the burner, she holds it in the air. A thick coating of burnt java rims the bottom with little bubbles popping up like roofing tar.

"Darn-it," Candy sighs.

Trying to think who could be so stupid, she realizes it had been her. She must've forgotten to turn the machine off when Toth appeared.

Dumping a scoop of ice, salt, and a lemon into the glass pot, Candy swishes the remedy around, watching as the crud loosens and falls.

Feeling grumpy, she wonders if a touch of cabin fever has infested her again. After all, for the past two weeks the temperatures have been spring like, then all of a sudden, with no warning, a cold snap blows in, settling over Mongoose Falls.

What she needs is a breath of fresh air, maybe go for a stroll tonight. But by the time she bundles up, she'll be so bulky it'll be hard to walk.

Candy Jane longs to get out of Mongoose Falls, Minnesota, forever. Every time she tries to leave though, a setback happens. Her car breaks down, or she'll make excuses that she doesn't have enough money. Being honest with herself, Candy Jane has to admit; she's never tried that hard to get out of the small town. After all, it is home.

Glaring at the swooshing revolving door as a family of six rolls in, Candy feels a pit grow in her gut. The father has two small children dangling from his arms, with another sleeping in a car seat. Following is his wife. Her arms filled with another child and a diaper bag.

Shaking her head, Candy begins setting a table for them.

❊   ❊   ❊

Hector Toth spies through the greasy kitchen window after ducking behind the door. Leering, he sees Candy Jane push Billy away from her. That's a good sign, he smiles, holding his breath. Could she be coming to her senses? Toth's fantasies ignite.

He's been in love with Candy Jane for about six months now, and craves her more than ever. They've known each other since childhood, as most of the residents in Mongoose Falls do. Then, out of the blue, he begins to see her in a different light. As if cupid has stung him with an arrow. Giggling, he recalls the day she bumped into him accidentally. He was electrified, she groveled.

That's when he decided Candy Jane Cane will be the mother of his children. Nobody knows of his obsession, and no one will. There will be the perfect time, Hector believes, when Candy will realize how much she desires him.

Feeling his intestines twist as Billy kisses Candy Jane on the cheek, Toth sneers as his competition heads out the door. Glancing back at Candy, he watches as she opens another box of Fruit Loops. Shaking some into her mouth, she then stuffs the cardboard into her apron pocket. He'll have to remember to dock her paycheck. Turning away disheartened, Toth rushes back to his office, closing the door behind him.

"Hey Toth, you in there?" He barely has a chance to take a breath, before hearing again. "Hector."

Loud knocks follow the outcry.

At first he doesn't know who it is, but then recognizes the voice, as his stomach begins to churn at the idea of having to deal with Cynthia Scotchland. He hesitates in answering.

He and Cynthia were an item up until a couple of months ago. All Toth wanted was sex, and someone to have dinner with every now and then, and told her this from the beginning, but she kept insisting on more. So he broke it off, and had succeeded in avoiding her, until now.

Wrapping his sweaty palm around the doorknob, Toth turns it, and listens as a shallow clicking sound echoes off the peeling drab, brown walls. He shivers, as though someone has just walked over his grave. Swinging the door open, Toth steps forward.

"What do you want, Cynthia?"

Brushing past him, she stomps over to his desk. "Shut the door Toth. We need to talk, now!" She orders.

Not wanting to get into a confrontation, he does what he is told. Toth knows how she can get, and it isn't pretty. "There's nothing to talk about. I think I've made myself perfectly clear." His tone twangs in disgust.

She falls into him, and begins rubbing her body against his, trying to get a reaction. "I want you Hector, it's been such a long time, and it seems like you'd rather be by yourself, than with me." She pushes him away. Catching Toth by surprise, he stumbles backwards, stopping himself before slamming into the file cabinet.

Gathering his balance, he glares at her.

"Get out, it's over between us. You should've believed me when I told you it was only about sex, and nothing more. So let's just drop it, okay?"

Beaming her dark, black eyes at Toth, Cynthia barks. "There's someone else, isn't there?" She lunges toward him. "Isn't there?" She wails.

Hector edges around her. "No! Why can't you just get it

through your trailer-trash brain that I don't want anything to do with you."

"I know you're lying, and believe me, when I find out who she is, both of you are going to be sorry." Cynthia grinds her teeth, tightening her jaw like a madwoman.

"Hector, hey Toth." Candy Jane slips through the office door, immediately feeling the tension hanging in the air. Glancing at Cynthia, she thinks she recognizes her, but can't place the face. Looking back at Toth, she says. "Sorry if I'm interrupting anything, but Hector we need you up front. A bus load of older folks, heading for the casino, just shuffled in, and they're hungry and grouchy." She peers at the two standing silent. "So, whenever you get a chance." Her tone, sarcastic.

"I'll be there in a minute."

"You better make it a quick minute." Candy dashes away.

Slamming the door behind her, Cynthia rushes at Toth, screaming. "Is that her, huh Hector? Is she the woman you've been making love with? I saw how you looked at each other. I can smell the skank's scent on you."

"My gosh, Cynthia, calm down, she's just a waitress here, and not a very good one at that." His voice cracks.

"I can't believe this Toth, I thought you loved me."

"Hey, wait a minute, I never said anything about love, not once."

"You don't have to say it, I can feel it in the way we connect. The way you talk to me, and touch me."

"Listen Cynthia, I think the best thing for us to do is not

see each other at all. It'll make it easier for you."

Hector feels the hairs on the back of his neck stiffen, like troops called to attention. He watches as Cynthia's face turns red. For a minute, Toth imagines her head bursting into tiny shards, splattering brain and blood all over Sven's office.

"What do you mean, not see each other anymore?" Cynthia yells at the top of her lungs. "You can't just up and tell me that, I won't accept it."

"For one thing Cynthia, it's my life, and I can do what I want."

Anger gags her, and for a split second, by the look of hate in Cynthia's eyes, Toth pictures her attacking him. Instead, she stands taut, erect, and surprisingly, Hector feels his manhood twitch.

Turning around to the door, Cynthia flings it open. Twisting her head back so fast her hat falls to the floor, she curses at Toth.

"You'll be back, you just wait and see. I know men like you. Thinking you can go without a certain woman, but always coming back to them in time of need. Because, believe me, once that new slut of yours realizes what kind of man you really are, she'll dump you like the morning trash. Then we'll see who's bedpost you'll be knocking on."

Cynthia Scotchland, all five feet one inch of her, whips out the door and is about to slam it, when she pokes her pointy-head back in, and snips. "Mine!"

Hector exhales, as he hears her scampering steps hurrying down the dim hall. Shaking his head, his mouth creases with a slight grin. In a way, she's right.

Suddenly, Candy Jane careens around the corner yelping, "Toth, we need you out on the floor, now." Turning around, she vanishes into the shadows.

"Yeah, yeah, yeah!" He replies, skipping out of his office, exalted over Cynthia's threats.

❋   ❋   ❋

Billy Mendelson pops his Toyota Tundra into gear, spinning around on the snow packed parking lot of *Sven's All You Can Eat Smorgasbord*. Cars pulling in from the highway, swerve to avoid the truck figure-eighting across the ice.

"Yahoo, yahoo," he screams, reaching for a beer. Ripping the top off with the bottle opener attached next to his radio, Billy looks around before taking a long chug off the Bud. He has no problem drinking and driving. Especially in the boondocks, where the only thing you'll drive into is your own back yard. "Friggin' Mongoose Falls."

Billy hates it here, he's never been any further than Minneapolis, three hours south of this pit, and even that isn't very impressive. Everything's going to change though, after Candy Jane marries him. They'll take off, maybe head out to California, throw dust to the wind, or whatever that saying is. They'll settle down, have a couple of kids, and maybe, just maybe, he'll try to stop drinking, get his act together for his family. The insurance money from his dad's untimely death will help them get started. Now all he has to do is convince Candy to marry him.

Taking a deep swig off his beer, he tosses the empty bottle out the back window onto the truck bed. The brown glass disappears into the mounting layer of snow. Tearing out of the driveway and onto Route 9, Billy speeds toward town to get more brew before heading home.

Jamming the stick into third gear, he feels the trucks tires slide on the slick road. Yup, the town's socked in tonight. He hopes the roads will still be drivable when he has to pick up Candy.

Leaning closer to the windshield, Billy tries to see through the blizzard. Out of fun, he flicks the light switch off, then right back on, as he feels the Toyota slip. Even though Billy knows luck is on his side, he doesn't want to push it tonight.

Gale forces whip the cab back and forth, and for a brief instant Billy has no idea if he's on the road or not. Trying not to show himself any fear, he puts both hands on the wheel and steadies himself. For a second he thinks he sees something run across the road, but then brushes it off as his imagination.

Feeling slightly edged, Billy eases his foot off the accelerator. He knows it's just the storm messing with him. Trying to control his shaking hands, he focuses on the road, as sleeting snow slashes around him.

❄ ❄ ❄

Candy Jane's blood pressure is reaching an all time high. She can feel her pulse pounding out of her carotid artery.

Not only did more people squeeze through the door, but Jimmy has not shown up yet, and Toth is still MIA. Storming into the lounge for a quick second, while the herd begins to gather at the trough: Sven's buffets are always a hit with the locals and tourists, Candy jaunts up to the mahogany bar where Patricia, the bartender stands, and leaning over, begs. "Please, may I have a tequila? These customers are driving me nuts, and Jimmy's late."

With no hesitation, Patricia pours a shot of Jose Cuervo into a glass, and sets it in front of Candy. A slice of lime dangling from the rim.

"No salt, right?" Patricia confirms.

"Nope, takes the taste away."

Holding the glass up, Candy toasts to the air, squeezes the tangy fruit in her mouth, and downs the burning booze.

"Rahhh," Candy grunts, wiping her mouth with a napkin. "Thanks, Patricia."

Plopping down on the padded stool, she feels the air escape like a hidden fart. Laughing, Candy wishes she had another shot sitting in front of her, as she watches the slender Swiss bartender stock beer. Patricia is new to the area, and Candy knows little about her. She seems nice though, and never refuses her when she asks for a drink.

"Working a double today?" Patricia asks, her words laced with a Swiss-French accent.

"Yup, one of the waiters is sick, so I'm stuck here till eight."

"Here, maybe this will help." She places two shots on the table then picks one up. "To working a double." Patricia says, clinking Candy's glass, and downing the liquor. Candy follows, suddenly wishing she had not partaken in the second drink. She can already feel the alcohol go to her head.

Patricia scoops up the two glasses, but hesitates. Swallowing she asks. "So, who is that woman Toth was with early?"

"I think her name is Cynthia Scotchland. They used to be a thing, but Toth broke it off. I think he has the hots for someone else. I'll be praying for that woman."

"He's not that bad?"

"Right, wait till you get to know him." Candy pushes the chair back, and edges out. "Well, I guess I'd better get back before I decide to have another one."

"Just let me know." Patricia motions.

"How much do I owe you?"

"It's on Hector."

"Why you tell him, thank you very much." Feeling better, she digs into her pocket and pulls out a five. Slapping it on the bar, she says, "Thanks again, Patricia."

No sooner does she turn around, than Jimmy, who at last has decided to show up, wraps his arms around her and starts twirling. Sensing a purge surging, Candy wriggles out of his grasp.

"Please, let me go, you're making me sick." She pleads.

Setting Candy down, Jimmy studies her, and says, "Oh, sweetie, so sorry I'm late. It's the roads, they're terrible, and a girl can slip off them if she's not careful." Jimmy doing his May West impersonation.

Candy Jane smells booze, but isn't sure if it's him or her,

or the two of them. She scurries past Jimmy. "At least you're here, and I'm telling you right now, I'm leaving at eight no matter what happens."

"Yes, honey, anything you want."

"Right, you can start by dropping the drag queen act, and help me clear some plates away."

"My, my, aren't we testy."

"Shut up, Jimmy. I'm not in the mood."

Candy and Jimmy swoosh through the beaded doorway and out into the large dining room. "Man, when did all these people come in?"

"Right at five, three minutes after you called saying you'd be late."

"Hey, I'm sorry!" Jimmy smiles, and Candy suddenly knows it's wasn't the roads that delayed him.

Candy slaps him on the back, saying, "You dog, I know what kind of delaying you were doing."

Jimmy struts in front of Candy Jane, glancing back at her, he teases. "I don't kiss and tell." Flipping his handsome head around, Jimmy's caramel colored hair flutters in the streaking light.

"Who is he? The same guy you've been sneaking around with, for what, a month now. What's his name, you know, the married one."

Wrapping his arm around Candy, Jimmy nuzzles his nose into her neck. "Now, honey, discretion is the key to having an affair. I mean, even though you are my best friend, I can't tell you. And trust me, there are a lot of men in this one horse town who want me."

"Cane, Prescott." Turning their attention toward the kitchen, they see Toth rumbling out, screaming their names.

"My gosh, Hector." Jimmy voices. "You don't have to yell, we're standing right here, sweetie."

"That's the point. You're standing doing nothing, while tables need to be bussed, glasses refilled, and food served." Toth folds his arms across his chest.

Jimmy peers over to the group, and grins. "They don't look like they need any more food to me, that's for sure." He begins laughing to himself, and Candy Jane tries hard not to join him.

Glaring at Jimmy, Toth huffs away. "Just get to work."

Still laughing, Jimmy smacks Candy on the arm. "Come on, that was funny, and you know it."

"Yeah, it was kind of. But I'm not going to laugh at the customers while Toth is standing right here."

"Well, you're no fun." He grabs her hand. "Come on, let's go."

The two of them clear away what seems like tons of dirty plates with wasted food. The stream of people flow through-out the evening, even with the weather worsening. Candy Jane prays for the night to end, but whenever she looks at the clock, it reads six forty-five. She swears an hour goes by, yet time stands still.

Candy Jane yanks Jimmy's arm as he sweeps by her. "Hey, what does your watch say?"

"Does anyone have the time?"

"Come on, stop it." Candy is wound tighter than a top.

"Geeze, calm down." Shaking the jewelry down his

wrist, Jimmy raises his arm to look at it. "It's twenty to eight. You're almost out of here, Miss Cranky."

"You're a card." Candy snaps at him.

"Yes, I know, the Queen of Hearts."

Candy can't help but giggle. "Listen, I'm going to stop taking tables. The place is emptying, and by the looks of it outside, I don't think we'll see many more people tonight."

"Yeah, why don't you get your raggedy ass outta here."

"Why, thanks for making me feel better, but I'll take you up on that. First, I'm getting a drink." Candy meanders to the bar and hears the slight steps of Jimmy following behind.

"Hey, wait for me." He squeals. Seeing Patricia, he dashes over and lifts her in a gigantic bear hug.

"My word, it's not as though you two haven't seen each other in years, you've been working together all night." Candy shakes her head and reconsiders staying.

"Yes, but we didn't get a chance to hug."

"Oh, hell." Candy slides onto a stool, deciding to have a quick one. If Jimmy ever lets Patricia go.

Scowling at Candy, he sets her down, and Patricia quickly scurries behind the bar, a little embarrassed by Jimmy's actions. She eyes Candy. "The same as earlier?" The Swiss asks.

Suddenly, Candy Jane feels slightly uncomfortable, as her voice quivers when replying. "Yes, please, and a Corona."

Jimmy saddles up next to Candy Jane, and she nudges him for some space. "Hey, sorry about the horn dog, Patricia. I swear, you could give him a donut and he'd be happy."

"Hey, don't talk about me while I'm sitting right here, at least not until I've had a cocktail." He flutters his eyes at Patricia.

Instinctively, she reaches behind her, and grabs the Jack Daniel's bottle, sailing the amber liquor into the glass setting on the bar.

"You're good!" Jimmy exclaims, as she places it in front of him. He spins his chair to face Candy. "To you, my little chickadee."

"Cheers!" They clinked glasses. Candy Jane sips this drink, squeezing lime in her mouth after every swallow. She watches Jimmy down his in one gulp.

"Should we have a quick smoke?" He gasps.

"Sure." Candy Jane replies, striking a match, as Jimmy places a cigarette between his lips. She hears the tobacco sizzle, as he inhales and then blows out a stream of blue-gray smoke. Taking another drag, he hands the fag to her.

"So what's the matter?" Jimmy inquires, taking the cigarette back. "You've been a little testy all night, and I know it's not about you having to work." Another quick puff. "So the only other thing that causes you grief, is Billy." He tries to hand the coffin-nail back, but Candy Jane declines, feeling the slight head rush of the nicotine.

"You know me so well."

"So what happened?"

"Nothing really, the same crap. He shows up drunk, and expects me to drop what I'm doing just because he's horny. Nope, it doesn't work like that. He's beginning to get a little possessive, and that scares me."

"Scares you, and me. You've been sleeping with him for three years now. How, I have no idea. Maybe he's looking for something more than just the occasional romp."

"If that's what Billy is searching for, then he's sniffing in the wrong place." Candy finishes the rest of her drink as Jimmy orders two more. "I don't know if I have time for another one, Jimmy." Candy protests.

"Ah, just one more. Now, go on."

"Well, ya know, I want something else in a man, I want to feel a spark, a tingle, a heart palpitation, when I see my guy. Not this nausea every time I think of Billy."

"So, you mean he's not going to be the father of your children?" Jimmy jokes.

Pretending to gag, Candy punches Jimmy in the arm. "Hell no, and there's never been any question when it came to that. I'd get an IUD, use the sponge, diaphragm and pill, all at the same time, while making Billy wear six condoms, if there was ever the slightest chance of me getting pregnant."

Jimmy chuckles. "Well, the rubbers might enhance his endowment." This sends the two of them hollowing, as Patricia eases over, trying to quiet them before Toth hears. After calming down, Jimmy says, still sniffling with laughter. "Wait here, I'm going to see if anyone new came in."

He disappears for a moment, returning quickly. As he sits back down, Candy asks. "Hey, Jimmy, do you want to hear this dream I had last night?"

"Sure, why not."

"I'm sitting in the plaza by the bandstand with all of these people from town, except I don't recognize anyone. We're all staring up at the sky because we think a plane is going to crash, but as it gets closer, everyone realizes that it is a brown horse with one of its legs cut off. The leg is falling beside the horse. When it hits the ground, it splatters, and in a craze, the crowd rushes over to the mangled torso and begins eating off of it. They are devouring it so fast that meat is being flailed back at me, and it feels like I'm breathing it in."

"Man, you're sick." Jimmy moans. "What in the hell did you eat before you went to bed, a can of Purina?"

"Ha ha, you're so funny."

Jimmy surveys the room, making sure no one is in ear shot, he leans closer to Candy Jane and whispers. "Hey, do you want to know what I dreamt about last night?"

"No, not really." She teases. "I'm sure it's something sexual."

"I dreamt me and Toth were making it together."

"Oh gross, and you say my dreams are sick."

As if on cue, they hear a slight squeak of the kitchen door as it opens. Downing their drinks, they slip a tip on the bar for Patricia, and hurry back to the dining room. By the tension in Hector's face, he's in no mood for goofing off.

Marching up to the two of them as they pretended to be busy, he orders. "Cane, punch out. Prescott, you're staying until we close at nine."

Jimmy peers outside and notices the storm getting worse. The snow now falling in a straight white sheet. "It seems like it's getting pretty messy out there, Hector."

"Yeah, and so?"

"Don't you think it might be a good idea if we close early. I bet you there aren't going to be many people daring the roads tonight, and I'm sure the crew wouldn't mind getting out of here before conditions become more treacherous."

At first Candy Jane thinks Toth is going to scream at Jimmy, like he did the other day in the store room. It was the first time in their tense working relationship that he has ever gotten hostile toward her. Instead, he glances out the window, and says. "We'll see what it's like at eight-thirty."

Toth's tone catches Jimmy off guard, as he opens his eyes wide in surprise. "Okay, Hector." Jimmy lisps. "I'll come find you then, and we can decide what to do." He bats his eyelids, like Doris Day.

Candy can't believe Jimmy is coming on to Toth. Good thing Hector doesn't have a clue, otherwise Jimmy would be lifting himself out of a snow bank. Without saying another word, Hector disappears into the kitchen.

Tugging Candy's arm, he rushes her over to the front door with him. "Quick, let's put the *Closed* sign up."

She laughs at Jimmy's vagary. "What if Toth sees it?"

"He won't. He's oblivious to details like that. We're the ones who always turn the board anyway." Jimmy pauses. "Plus, he'll be so mesmerized by me, he won't notice anything else."

"Let me make a suggestion, Jimmy. Be careful with Toth. I don't think he's the kind of guy who'd take another man flirting with him, ya know?"

"Yeah, yeah! You'd be surprised how many men want Mr. Johnson. The statistics are staggering."

"Believe me, Toth isn't one of those statistics."

Dismissing Candy's warning, Jimmy says. "I think I could use another drink before we start breaking things down."

"We? What's this *we* crap?"

"Hey, I figured since you're leaving, and I'm gonna be here till the wee hours of the morning, that out of the kindness of your heart, you'd want to help me clean up."

"I'll help a little, but I don't want another drink."

"At least keep me company."

"Okay, but let's make it fast. I've been here long enough."

They ramble through the swinging red velvet door, leading to the speakeasy style lounge at, *Sven's All You Can Eat Smorgasbord*.

❀　❀　❀

"Oh, no!" Billy snips, jumping out of bed and reaching for the phone. "Damn-it!" He's gonna be late picking up Candy Jane. Now, he has to call, deal with her mood, and tell her he'll be right there. He'll explain that he fell asleep, which he did, but Candy will accuse him of passing out. How many times have they replayed this scenario?

Maybe he can sweet talk Candy into driving over here. Tell her his mom's gone for the evening, so they'll have the place to themselves. Promise he won't drink, or at least, not get drunk.

Tapping number three on the speed dial, Billy lays back on his pillow, listening to the tin-can sounding ring. He outlines the cowboy figures on his sheets with his finger as he waits. It seems to be taking forever, they can't be closed yet, Billy ponders, glancing at his digital watch.

His head is pounding, as fierce winds whip wildly at the frost bitten windows. Billy is just about to hang up, when a crackling voice comes over the line.

"Hello."

"Um, oh yeah, hey dude. Um, let me talk to Candy Jane."

Billy hears a ruckus in the back ground, and then the foreign voice comes back on the line.

"She's a little busy right now."

"What do you mean busy, she's supposed to be done at eight."

"I don't know what to tell you." The voice sounds curt. "Can I take a message?"

"Yeah, tell her Billy called, and I won't be picking her up, so just come over to my house, but get some beer first." He hangs up before she has a chance to reply. "Damn-it," he hisses, grabbing a Bud out of his cooler.

"How much longer do I have to wait to get laid?" Billy asks himself, hoping that by now, Candy Jane would be getting ready to go home, not just be arriving.

Running his hand through his dirty red hair, a noxious scent stings his nostrils, and shaking his head, Billy knows Candy Jane will have nothing to do with him, smelling like this.

Displeased he has to shower when it's so cold out, Billy swings his legs over the side of the bed, and stands up. A quick rinse will do it, he grumbles to himself.

Shimmying out of his sweats, he sniffs them, and turning his face away, throws the sodden gray pants across the room. They melt down the wall like a fainting shadow.

Yanking his tank-top off, he ruffles the orange, fuzzy patch of hair on his chest. Creeping across the frigid floor, Billy sneaks into the shower, standing under the steaming stream of water jetting rapidly from the breast shaped nozzle.

Yup, he certainly *is* the ladies man, he dreams, wishing more than ever that Candy will show up. Heat fills his taunt body, and Billy feels like just ending his misery now. But he'll wait, it'll just be that much better with Candy.

Fiddling with the faucets, he turns the hot water off, and twists the cold onto high. His shrill voice screams, as coldness coats his shrinking phallus.

Grabbing the Irish Spring from the soap dish, he lathers the bar and rubs it all over. Quickly finishing, Billy bends over to turn off the water, and stepping out, leaves the shower curtain open so his mom can see the tub needs to be cleaned.

Retreating back into the bedroom, he picks up the still cold brew and hears behind him. "Hey, big boy!"

Billy jumps at the voice. Turning around, and remembering he's still naked, he glares at the figure sitting in the corner chair toasting him with one of his precious Budweiser's.

"What the hell?" He screams, slamming his beer down on the plywood dresser, regretting the act the minute the brew starts to foam over.

"Calm down sweetie," she says, standing up and slithering over to Billy. In one svelte move she thrust her tongue down his throat. Feeling her hand reach down and strike gold, Billy knows he should stop her, even though he's inclined not to.

Pushing Cynthia away, he screams in pain as she rakes her pointed fingernails across his bare chest. "Damn-it, Cynthia, what do you think you're doing?"

Moving a step closer, as Billy edges back, she taunts him. "Come on, Billy Boy, I know you want me, and always have." She charges toward him as he stumbles on his heels.

"Stay away from me, and get the hell out of my house, you crazy bitch." Billy yells, trying to fend off her advances.

Stopping in her tracks, she razor stares her prey. "Well, you're gonna change your tune, once I tell you what I found out." She chimes.

Billy reaches down and grabs yet another pair of dirty sweats from his bed. Man, his mom is really slacking off. Stuffing himself into them, Billy sneers at Cynthia.

"What are you talking about?"

"Toth and Candy."

"You're not making sense."

Scrunching her face, Cynthia spits. "Your precious little girlfriend is screwing Hector Toth."

"You're insane." Billy searches for a shirt.

"Oh yeah, just see for yourself." She reaches into her

pocket and pulls out a picture, handing it to Billy.

At first, he doesn't know what he's looking at until he holds it closer. "This is bullshit." He flings the photo back at Cynthia. "It's a fake."

"No, it's real, I took it myself."

"When?"

"Tonight! Candy Jane didn't have to work, she stayed late to be with Toth."

Billy pushes past her, reaching for his beer on the nightstand. "You're a lying skank."

"Am I?"

Billy feels rage rush over him, his body fuels with fire. Grabbing Cynthia, he begins kissing her harshly on the lips. His clumsy hands grope for her skirt, tearing it off, he notices she has nothing on beneath.

Turning Cynthia around, he bends her over his desk chair, nailing her like a hammer to wood. "Oh, oh Cindi, you were right, you feel so good. Oh, baby."

He begins pumping faster and faster as Cynthia moves along with him, pretending to be enjoying his rabbit movements. Giving her one last thrust, he stills for an instant until his body spasms. Ripping himself out of her, he falls backwards onto the bed. "Oh, my," he gasps. "What in the hell did you do to me?"

"It's a secret." She teases. "I'm not finished with you yet." Strutting over to him, she hands him his beer. "Here, finish this first." Smiling, Cynthia's surprised at how quickly the crushed Viagra, she laced his drink with, is working. Crawling on top of his hardened body, Billy Mendelson can't believe he's ready to fire again, as Cynthia Scotchland slides down on him.

❀   ❀   ❀

Sheriff Jon Anderson sits in the living room trying not to doze off as he listens to his wife finishing up the dishes in the kitchen. She's been in there for the past hour, and to him, that seems like a long time. For some reason he feels like she's avoiding him, but doesn't know why.

Her queer behavior started a couple of weeks ago, when she began disappearing before he'd get home. The only reason she probably didn't go out tonight is because of the weather.

"Maybe at last I can get to the bottom of this," he whispers to himself, watching her shadow on the door as it reaches up and hangs a pan.

Glancing up at the Coo-Coo clock placed above the mantel, Jon admires the fireplace he and Carol built together, rock by rock. They'd planned on raising a family, but Carol couldn't conceive, so the two of them have lived in this large house by themselves for twenty-one years. John loves the space, but obviously, Carol is feeling a little cramped.

Closing his eyes, Jon recaps his day. The only incident was with that Bryant boy who was skate boarding on the sidewalk. All Jon wanted to do was give the kid a warning, but he skated off, flicking Jon the finger as he disappeared down an alley.

"There's just no respect, these day," he mutters.

Strolling in from the kitchen, Carol asks. "What did you say?" She continues to wipe her hands on the blue-striped dish towel.

"Nothing." He replies, rolling off the couch, like a bear from a rock. "You all done?" He wraps his arms around her, nuzzling her cheek.

Gently pushing him away, she responds. "Yes, with the dishes, but now I have to make a cake for the grade school bake sale tomorrow."

"Bake sale, why are you baking one?"

"I volunteered."

Shaking his head, and sitting on the couch, Jon says. "I just don't get it."

"There's nothing to get Jon, I like participating, it keeps me busy. Plus, I enjoy being around children, they make me feel alive, not stifled."

"Now you're being stifled?"

"No, you're taking this the wrong way, and I can tell which direction this conversation is heading, so let's just drop it. Okay?"

"I don't want to drop it. You've been acting strange lately, and I want to know what's going on."

"There's nothing going on, Jon. I just feel like I need to make a few changes, do something invigorating so that I can start growing again."

Rising quickly, Jon sweeps his arm around the living room. "This isn't stimulating? Our life, our home, me?"

Carol Anderson looks at her husband longingly, "Yes, Jon it is. I just feel I need some outside inspiration. You don't understand." Carol snaps as she retreats back to the kitchen, leaving Jon mesmerized in her wake.

"What the hell." He yelps. "Carol, get back here." He half orders, knowing she won't respond.

Baffled over the turn of events, Jon thinks about going down to the station and finishing up some paper work, but then reconsiders as he hears the winds howling from outside. It would be crazy to go out in this weather, instead, he decides to lock himself up in his study and watch some TV. If Carol wants to talk, she knows where to find him.

"I'm busy, I'm busy," Candy Jane waves her hands at Patricia, signaling she doesn't want to talk to Billy right now. The slim bartender understands, it's not the first time she's had to lie.

"Billy wants you to go over to his house instead of him coming to pick you up." She relays the message to Candy.

"Thanks, Patricia." Turning toward Jimmy, Candy grumbles. "Billy's nuts if he thinks I'm going to drive clear across town in this storm."

"I thought you wanted to see him tonight."

"Part of me does, but the other part just wants to go home."

"Then you should go with your gut." He takes a sip of his Tom Collins, having switched cocktails midstream. "You know, Miss Cane, I have a couple of friends I can set you up with, they'd really be into you."

"Oh, no, we're not going there. I'm not into women at all, so don't start up." Candy grunts.

"See, you all ready know how to cough up a fur ball."

Candy punches him in the arm.

"Ouch!' Jimmy whines. "The point of the matter is, you need to have a new yacht docked in your slip, if you get my drift."

"Nothing like a little phallic symbolism." Candy Jane snorts. Grabbing her tip bucket, she spills the money onto the bar. A pile of change clanks against the wood, as dirty, green dollar bills flutter on top.

"Slim pickens, I'd say." She grabs a handful and begins straightening the money out, heads on heads.

Peeling through the contaminated currency, Candy sneers, "Man, I can't live on this."

Jimmy gleams at her. "What'd you make?"

"A little over sixty bucks."

"Ouch! For ten hours?"

"There should be a mandatory restaurant etiquette class before anyone can go out to eat. Yeah know, teach these ya-whoos the rights and wrongs of the business."

"That'd be the day." Jimmy lights another cigarette and hands it to Candy, she shakes her head no, still feeling sick from the first one.

"Listen, I think I'm going to cruise. I'm beat, and the roads are getting pretty bad." Candy slips out of her seat.

Placing his hand on her arm, Jimmy asks. "So, what are you going to do?"

"About what?"

"Billy?"

"I don't know. Go home, get a good night's sleep, and then see how I feel in the morning. That's about all."

"You can do better."

"I know, but there's just something about him."

"You're the only one who sees it."

Becoming slightly annoyed at Jimmy's constant Billy bashing, Candy Jane snaps. "Hey, lay off him, you don't know the man, and tonight you're going a little too far with your Sinicism."

"All right, all ready. What's the big deal, I'm just joking, you're being way too sensitive."

Reaching into her apron pocket, Candy Jane pulls out the box of Fruit Loops she's been eating, and nervously shoves some in her mouth. It's like she's addicted to them.

Unhooking her orange parka from the coat rack, she slips her arms through the gaudy downed mass. "I'm outta here."

"You're not going to help me clean up?"

"No."

"Good, then take your snooty attitude home." Sarcasm laces Jimmy's words, and she tries to ignore him, knowing the booze is starting to hit.

"Prescott, go home." A booming voice waves over them before they see Toth stampede through the lounge door. "We're closing, so finish up."

"Thanks, Hector, any plans for after work?"

"Not with you."

"Prick." Jimmy curses under his breath.

"You're certainly a piece of work. I'll see you later."

Candy Jane heads toward the entrance, but hears Jimmy's footsteps padding behind her.

"Hey, wait, Candy Jane, I'm sorry, sometimes I don't know what gets into me."

"I do. Too much sauce." Candy says. "Be careful out there, Jimmy, and I'll see you tomorrow." She kisses his cheek.

"Bye."

Candy thinks Jimmy looks like a wounded puppy, but also knows it's a ploy used quite frequently. She wheels through the screeching century old door, bracing herself before it spits her out into the frigid night air. Snowy winds whip her face as Candy lowers her head and tightens her hood.

Opening the unlocked car, she stuffs herself in. Her coat is so big it squishes against the steering wheel. Turning the key, the engine roars to life. "Nothing like a new battery," Candy tells herself, sitting there shivering, waiting for the heat to kick in and windows defrost.

For a brief instant, Candy considers going to Billy's, but then decides otherwise. The blizzard is getting much worse, and tonight she just wants to be in her own bed. She'll call him from home.

Grinding the gear into first, she removes the emergency brake, and slowly inches forward. Flicking the lights on, she switches the wipers to fast, and listens as the rubber blades crunch against the frozen windshield. Hanging on tight to the steering wheel as the vicious winds attack her, Candy Jane slowly eases away.

❋ ❋ ❋

Billy Mendelson awakes with a start, and at first, doesn't know where he is. Ruffling his hair, he moves his hand down his body to where he feels sore and achy. Jolting up, he surveys the room. Where is she?

Rolling his legs over the bed, Billy groans, "Damn, what did that bitch do to me?" He mumbles, picking the alarm clock up off the floor and glimpsing the time. "And where the hell is Candy Jane?"

Bending over and reaching from his pants, Billy groans as a sharp cramp creases his midsection. Maybe it's best if Candy Jane doesn't come over tonight. He hurts so bad, Billy doesn't think he can perform again.

The ringing phone rattles his fuzzy brain. Picking up the receiver, he chokes out.

"Hello."

"Billy? Hey Billy is that you."

Covering the mouth piece with his hand, he hacks, then replies, "Yeah, hey Candy Jane, what's up?"

"What's wrong with your voice?"

"Oh, nothing, I just did a bong, and almost coughed out a lung. My throat is really raw."

"That's real healthy." Candy hesitates. "Hey, I think I'm going to stay home this evening. The roads are getting pretty bad, and I don't want to be out. You won't be mad, will you?"

The throbbing ceases slightly, but still, there's no way he wants any more sex tonight. "No, that's fine. I don't want you taking any risks, so just stay put." Relief overwhelms him.

Put off by his quick response, Candy wonders what he's up to, and asks. "What are you doing?"

"The usual. Laying around, getting high and having a couple of beers." He waits for a sarcastic sting, but nothing comes across the line. "So, why are you calling me so late?"

"I just got home. I haven't even taken my coat off yet. Give me a break."

Billy hears a tightness in Candy's voice and tries to ease her down. "I'm worried, that's all." Tired of talking, Billy attempts to get off the line. "Why don't we plan for tomorrow, okay. You sound exhausted. I'll call you in the morning."

"Billy, can you try not to be drunk?"

"I can try." He says, trying to be funny.

"I'm serious."

"Well, then let's get together early." Chuckling.

"You're unbelievable. I'm gonna go. Good night, Billy."

"Night, Candy."

Billy listens as the phone clicks, and then a moment of crackling static. He hangs up, as a growing concern waxes over him.

Candy Jane snuggles deeper beneath her down comforter as she stares out the bedroom window watching the storm mount. Amelia bounds up behind her head, and tramples across the pillow to the other side, the cat's new sleeping spot. Reaching out, she pets the feline, her short orange fur soft to the touch.

Billy's acting weird, she thinks. He's up to something, but she can't figure out what. She knows eventually she'll get to the bottom of it, but tonight all she wants to do is lay here in bed and not think about anything or one.

Flicking off the silent television, a quiet darkness fills the room, until the brightness of the snow from outside illuminates the walls into a soft white. Candy hears the tiny pellets of sleet click against the aluminum siding. A familiar and comforting sound. Closing her eyes, sleep comes quickly as Candy slips into her dreams.

Mira Mendelson hears the phone ring, but doesn't answer it, figuring it's for her son. Plus, she doesn't want Billy to know she's home yet. He'll undoubtedly have something to complain about, or a chore for her to do as if she's his personal maid. Mira loves him dearly, but it's getting too be time for Billy to start thinking about moving out.

Pouring water into the tea kettle, she sets it on the stove, igniting a small flame beneath the pot. Sighing deeply, Mira wishes the weather hadn't gotten so bad. The Mongoose Falls Book Club was just getting going when they all agreed to call the meeting due to the snow.

The group of six women have been gathering now for little over a year, and the camaraderie between them is strengthening. Especially with Carol Anderson. They used to be best friends when they were younger, early high school years, but then they had a falling out, and their friendship just kind of dissolved. Mira can't recall if it was over a boy or not.

At first Mira hesitated joining the club. She's more or less become a hermit after her husband, Stanley, died five years ago. It was a freak accident, some whispered suicide. It's quite feasible for a painter to get tangled in a rope, fall and hang himself.

"This town just wants something to gossip about," she believes.

Even now, it surprises Mira how little she feels. Is she a bad person just for thinking that?

Their marriage was okay, more disappointing than anything. He never laid a hand on her, but boy did he drink. Mira figures that is where Billy gets it from. He, being the biggest let down of her life.

The kettle begins to whistle and Mira quickly turns the flame off, hoping Billy doesn't hear the shrill. Listening for a minute, she hears nothing, and continues making herself a cup of tea. Tip-toeing to her bedroom, she gently closes her door, making sure it's shut tight before turning on the light.

Maybe she should ask Carol out to dinner some night. It doesn't seem like she has many friends, either, Mira contemplates. Who knows, there might be a chance the two of them can try to rekindle their acquaintance of so many years ago.

A lightness fills Mira as she lays down and watches the drifting snow. It's stopped falling, but now as the temperatures dip, and the winds become more severe, Mira's glad she's home.

❋   ❋   ❋

Hearing a noise downstairs, Billy figures it's his mom, and turns out his light, hoping she doesn't come and bother him. He's not in the mood to listen to one of her boring stories about the *Book Club*. His mind races as he lays back down, and reaching for a beer in the cooler next to his bed, opens it and drinks thirstily.

Candy's suspicious, he senses it. Can tell by the doubt in her voice. Billy knows how clever she is, and when she finds out, that will be the end to them. He feels sick. What came over him? It's as though Cynthia sprayed herself with those pheromone perfumes. He's heard they're supposed to make you real horny, and it certainly worked on him.

Snickering, he rolls over in agony as a pain jabs his groin. This is no laughing matter, he believes, leaning his head on the back board. Closing his eyes he suddenly feels tired, and sets his beer down on the stand. He'll finish the brew in the morning.

❋   ❋   ❋

Hector Toth opens the door to his double wide, still astounded at how Candy Jane can be so blind to his feelings. How much more open does he have to be? Sniffing, he smells an odd odor, but puts it off as the trash.

Stepping into the dark kitchen and opening the fridge, he is squirted in the eye with a stream of bright light. Dazzled, he blindly reaches for a PBR, and grabbing one, closes the door behind him. Blue flecks float in the air as he listens to the snow filled gales whip and howl against his tin box trailer.

He has to figure out how to get Candy's attention; a way that she'll notice him. But what? Cupping his face in his hands, he shakes his head as the incident with Cynthia earlier replays in his brain.

Gosh, he wishes she would leave him alone. That's one of the things that drove him batty to begin with, her neediness, and how she clung to him, making him feel suffocated.

So what if she has issues with her past. It's not his problem that she had an abusive childhood, and plus, how much of what she says is true? Taking a pull off his beer, Toth smells that stench again, and this time wonders where it's coming from.

Switching on the light, Hector notices muddy foot prints on his clean floor, bee-lining for the pantry. Tip-toeing across the white Formica, he wraps his hands around the accordion closet door handle, and rips it open.

Empty?

"Damn it, Cynthia, if you're here, come out. I'm not in the mood for games." Racing through the house, Hector flicks on every light. He senses her lurking right in front of him. Hiding behind a curtain, a chair, a shadow.

"Cynthia!" He screams. Charging into the bathroom, Toth wisps his arm across the shower curtain, pulling the rod out of its holder. "Now, I'm really pissed," he growls, throwing the pole and curtain against the wall. Glancing out of the small window, and into the snowy distance, he sees a pair of frosted red-tail lights disappearing into the darkness.

"God damn-it." He curses, whipping his beer bottle into the tub. "I'm gonna kill that little bitch," Toth swears. "If it's the last thing I do."

Tramping back to the living room, Hector plops hard into his chair, and tries to calm down. A sparkle by the front door catches his attention, and he walks over to it. Getting closer, he recognizes it as being Cynthia's rhinestone scarf she wore earlier.

Picking it up, he stomps outside and throws it in the fire barrel. Spraying the garment with lighter fluid, Hector strikes a match and tosses it into the pit, backing away as the flames kiss his brow. "Take that, you sleazy tramp."

Jogging back to the trailer, he shuts the cheap, metal door against the winter winds. Just as he latches the lock, the lights flicker, and then total darkness. "Great," Hector groans. "This night just keeps getting better and better."

Loading the pot belly stove, he starts a fire easily. Hector, opening another beer, sits close to the heat, waiting for a calm to over take him.

❂ ❂ ❂

Cynthia Scotchland feels something snap in her head as she runs further from Toth's house, away from his screaming voice. Reaching her car without falling, she starts the brown Corolla and feels her wheels spin as she peels onto the highway.

"Dagnabit." She yells, waving her fist in the air. She's not done with Hector yet. She'll teach him a lesson, one he'll never forget.

Laughing to herself, she leans closer to the windshield,

trying to see the road before her. Maybe she'll tell Toth that she screwed Billy Mendelson, make him really jealous. Cynthia thinks about Billy with a dissatisfied taste in her mouth.

Seeing the flashing motel sign up ahead, Cynthia is relieved as she nears her home.

She's been staying in an efficiency for over a month now, after her stepfather kicked her out of her mom's. Nobody knows, not even Toth. She used an alias when she checked in, not wanting to be found by anyone. It's a nice enough room, a little kitchenette, bath and bed. The owner keeps it really clean too, which Cynthia enjoys. Seeing she hates messes.

Crawling into the parking lot, Cynthia turns off her lights, not wanting to draw any attention to herself. It's bright enough outside so she can see where she's going. Pulling around to the back, she slips out of her car, bracing herself against the winds.

Tomorrow she'll return to Toth's and reveal her conquest.

❂   ❂   ❂

Jimmy Prescott cringes as he turns into his driveway and watches the lights flicker out. "Shit," he yelps, banging his palms against the steering wheel. Now what is he going to do? He steers the red Tacoma into the car port and gets out, scrambling around in his pocket for the house keys.

Finding them, he opens the door, then leaning over, grabs a few little logs from the wood pile, almost dropping the six pack of Miller High Life into the snow. He'd be shit out of luck if he let those fall.

The harsh gales push Jimmy inside and the screen door slams him from behind. He stands panting for a moment, trying to let his eyes adjust. Setting the beer down, he bounds over to the fireplace, dumping the logs onto the stoop. One rolls off and hits his shin, sending waves of electric vibes rippling through his nerves.

"Ah, fudpucker!" He curses, jumping up and down, trying to rub the pain from his bruising leg. Bending over, he picks up the stray, and tosses it into the fireplace. It'll be the first to burn.

Prepping the kindling, he strikes a match and lights the paper. The dry splinters catch quickly, and before he knows it, Jimmy's feeling all comfy and cozy. Plopping down in the Laz-E-Boy chair, he tilts back, and twists open a beer. This is nice, he contemplates, a little peace and quiet for a change.

Patricia Moldine grits her teeth as she ducks from the oncoming headlights. The vehicle whizzes by her dark car parked on the side. Was it that Scotchland woman? Good thing she pulled over for a moment, otherwise she would've been hit.

Deciding not to go over to Toth's tonight, Patricia turns right instead of going straight to his place. She wants to surprise him, tell him of her feelings for him, but the weather is turning into her nemesis, and the safest thing to do is go home. Love can wait until tomorrow.

2

Morning awakes in Mongoose Falls, muffled quiet by the mounds of snow. Candy Jane rolls over, feeling a little sick to her stomach. Bunching the comforter closer to her chin, she pulls her legs up against her chest. Amelia, asleep at the foot of the bed, slaps at the mound, aggravated that she's been woken up.

Patting the space next to her head, Candy coos at the kitty. "Come here, baby, let Mommy give you a good morning kiss."

Meowing, Amelia stands, stretches and saunters up to Candy Jane. Sniffing her face, the cat bellows, and jumps off the bed.

"Fine, be that way." Rolling onto her back, she gazes at the ceiling. Thank goodness she doesn't have to work until four, *if,* the roads are passable. There's no way she's going to risk an accident for that two-bit job.

Curious as to how much snow fell, Candy whips the covers off, and dashes to the window. Snapping the drapes open, she gawks at the drifts that are as high as the shed out back.

Her eyes soften to the pure beauty. Dark clouds hover above the virgin white fields. Six acres of an untouched icy frontier. She wants to go play in it, jump up and down, fall backward into an angel, like she did as a kid. She knows she won't go out, though, it's all just a nice memory.

Confident that Sven's will be closed today, Candy feels calm and relaxed. A quiet day at home will do her a world of good, maybe she should just call Billy and say she has a fever.

A sharp pain inches its way across the front of Candy's brain. She rubs her hand along it, trying to ease the pounding. She knows that last shot of tequila with Jimmy was a bad idea. Just thinking of it makes her want to vomit.

Deciding a couple of Advil might help, she pulls the bottle off the shelf above the sink, twists it open, and shakes two into her mouth, swallowing them easily. She needs to take a break from drinking, it's starting to become a little too much. She doesn't even enjoying it anymore, it's more like a habit, a routine, that needs to be changed.

But can she do it?

Candy Jane opens the cupboard and eases the can of Folgers out. Filling the filter with ground beans, she pours water into the reservoir, and turning the switch on, hears the Mr. Coffee Machine gurgle to life.

An aroma fills the kitchen, bitter sweet, tantalizing

Candy's instincts. Even before having a cup, she feels a little more awake. She likes the familiarity she gets from this morning ritual, and recalls her dad having the same practice. That's where she must have gotten it from.

Decades have passed since Candy's dad split, and she still misses him. Her parent's just couldn't get along. Not only did he leave, though, he disappeared, seldom coming around after his emancipation.

The whole situation ended up putting a strain on her relationship with her mom, now, they seldom see or talk to each other.

Candy's heart races, as a cold shiver rakes across her body. She needs to get some heat going, there's a chill in the air, and the snow is starting up again.

Slipping into the living room and over to the fireplace, Candy crinkles up some paper balls and then tosses some dry kindling on top. Striking a match, she holds the tiny flame close, and then steps back as a small fire breaks free.

Stacking some larger logs on the blaze, Candy shuffles to the couch, and laying down, pulls the afghan over her body. Reaching for the remote on the floor, she aims the device at the Sony, clicks it, and watches as the television blitzes to life.

As usual, there's nothing on but talk shows, dull hosts trying unsuccessfully to be witty and cute. Switching the channel to 50, Candy smiles when she taps into a fuzzy episode of *Bewitched.*

Watching as Samantha twitches her nose and freezes everybody at a dinner party, Candy wishes she could petrify people. Or better yet, make them disappear. She can think of a couple right now she'd like to zap into nowhere land.

Muting a commercial, Candy closes her eyes and thinks about Billy. She's feeling a little bad about how she treated him last night. He really didn't deserve that. She knew before they got together how big of a drinker he is, but she still chose to get involved with him. And who is she to ask him to change?

She sees no future between them, and has been hoping lately that Billy will meet somebody else and then break up with her. It'd make things easier. She's not happy being with Billy anymore, and she needs to gather her guts and get out of the relationship herself. Candy knows there's no need in dragging it out any longer.

Billy awakes and reaches for his still aching groin. Sitting up, he looks at the digital clock. Bright red numbers silently bleep 10:11. Rubbing his face with his hands, he moans.

Why is he awake so early?

Wrapping his childhood blanket around his shoulders, he staggers to the bathroom, the cold floor boards beneath, numb his bare feet. Billy hears his mother shuffling around downstairs, and eases the door shut without a sound.

Washing his face and rinsing his mouth out, Billy can still smell the unpleasant scent of Cynthia clinging to his skin. Growing nervous at the prospect of Candy Jane finding out about last night, Billy races to his room, and dives back into his bed.

Making the sign of the cross over his chest, Billy grabs the phone, and presses the number one on his speed dial. He listens to the third ring, and then hears a gurgled voice come over the line.

"Hello."

"Hey, Candy Jane, that you?"

"Yes, Billy?"

"Are you still sleeping? I can call back later."

"No, no, I'm up, I must've dozed off." Candy glances out the window and notices the sun starting to peak through the clouds. Maybe she'll have to work after all. Disappointment fills her. She asks. "What's going on, Billy?"

"I'm just wondering what you're up too? You said you were going to call me today."

"My gosh Billy, I'm still trying to get going here, quit being so needy."

"I just thought you might want to go play in the snow."

Right now, the thought of hanging out with Billy Mendelson is the most unappealing idea she can think of.

"No, I'm still in my pajamas, plus, the roads aren't even plowed yet."

"That's okay, I can walk over."

"It's too far, Billy, don't be ridicules."

"Why, don't you want me to come over?" Billy sounds suspicious.

"I just need to spend some time alone, can you understand that?"

"Do you have someone else over there?"

"What?"

"You know what I'm talking about."

"Believe me, Billy, I haven't a clue."

"I know about you and Toth?"

"Me and who?"

"Hector Toth."

"What about him?"

"I know the two of you are doing it."

"You've got to be kidding. Where on earth did you come up with that?"

"I heard it through the grapevine."

"Well, let me tell you, that grapevine's producing sour grapes. There is no way in hell I would ever have sex with Toth. I can't even stand being in the same room with him. You need to censor the things you hear before telling me. Got it?" The line goes silent for a moment. "So, who told you this?"

"You don't know her, an old friend who's visiting from Minneapolis. I saw her at the bar yesterday."

"How does she know who I am."

"I showed her a picture of you. Now, can we drop it?"

"You're not making any sense."

"Why don't you just come over and we can talk about it." Billy whines.

"I can't come over till later. I have to work at four, so expect me at around three, okay?"

"Three, that's kind of late."

"What, you have plans?"

"I just thought we could spend a little more time together

than just forty-five minutes. You know, I haven't been seeing a whole lot of you lately, and I miss you." Billy feels more insecure than ever. "Plus, there's something I want to ask you."

"Ask me now."

"No, it's something I need to do in person."

Candy knows and fears his question. She has to beat him to the punch, and end it before he offers his hand in marriage. Can life be getting any more difficult?

"My mom's gonna be gone most of the day, so we can be alone, if you get my drift." Billy insinuates.

"Oh, I can't wait." Candy lies, a sudden tightness wrings her gut. "Where's your mom going?" Trying to change the subject.

"I don't know. She's probably doing some stupid thing with those old ladies she's been hanging out with."

"That's great Billy. It's about time she started getting out. No one saw her for years after your dad died, she more or less dedicated her life to you after that."

"Yeah, well you couldn't tell these days." Billy tries to joke. "Nothing's getting done."

Disgusted, Candy is curt. "She's your mom, not your maid, Billy. Golly, I tell you, sometimes I just don't get the things you say. Listen, I've gotta go, I'll see you around three."

"Hey, I'm just trying to be funny."

"Well, it's not working. Bye." Candy hangs up.

Studying the receiver, Billy wonders, what's gotten up her ass. He's the one who should be stressing out. He's about to propose.

Feeling hungry, Billy strolls down to the kitchen, where he finds his mom facing the stove. Pouring himself a cup of coffee, he mutters, "morning, Ma," and sits down at the table.

Mira turns to her only son. "Morning, Billy. You're up early today. Everything okay?"

If anything, Billy believes his mom is instinctual. "Ah, so, so. Me and Candy Jane are having a little disagreement."

"Oh?" Mira sets a plate of bacon and eggs in front of him, then turns to retrieve the toast that just popped up. "What about?" She continues.

"The usual. My life style, the drinking, my non-motivating behavior."

"Maybe you should think about working on those things, Billy. Candy Jane is such a nice girl, you don't want to lose her."

Put off by his mom's reaction, he wonders if today is going to be one of those, Billy bashing days. "Don't worry Mom, I have everything under control."

"Oh, do you, now?"

Holding up a piece of crisp bacon, Billy complains. "Come on Mom, you know I like mine on the raw side."

"Then cook it yourself." Mira snips back; she's growing tired of her sons attitude. "I'm on my way out, and I won't be home until later this evening, so you'll have to get your own meals. There's plenty of food, so don't worry."

Burdened with a little of that motherly guilt, Mira glides over to her son and kisses the top of his head. "I'm sure things will work out between you and Candy Jane."

"Thanks, Mom." The show of motherly comfort warms him.

Watching as she disappears down the hallway, Billy wishes she would get a life of her own, and quit harping on his. Things are going to get a little crowded around here once Candy moves in. Maybe he should start suggesting that it's time Mira thinks about living somewhere else so that he and his bride can have the house to themselves. Plus, it'll be good for her.

Wolfing down the rest of his food, he stands, burps, and trudges to the fridge. Opening it, he grabs the cartoon of orange juice, and drinks right out of the container. Leaving the plate on the table, Billy retreats to his room. He'll hang out there until after his mom leaves, then go down to the living room and watch *The Price is Right*.

Feeling thirsty, Billy takes inventory on his beer stock. He has about nine left. That should last him until after Candy leaves. Popping one open, he hears a knock, and stashing the can behind the mirror, opens the door.

His mother stands there with her eyes closed.

"Aw, come on, Mom, it's not that bad."

Mira raises her lids, and glances around her son's bedroom. She's seen worse. A slight scent of beer hangs in the air.

"Listen, Billy. I just want to apologize for this morning. I've been a little cranky lately, and I don't know why. Maybe it's a case of cabin fever. I just need to stay active."

"What you need to do is quit helping out those old folks

that you've become so attached to."

"They need help. I just hope that when I'm their age there's someone around for me." Mira eyes her son, but sees no reaction.

"I'm sure there will be Mom." Billy starts to close the door, but Mira stops him with her hand.

"If you need anything, I'm at Mrs. Abernathy's, okay."

"Thanks Mom, but I'm sure I'll be all right. Be careful out there." He tries to show some concern.

"I will." Mira turns and leaves as Billy closes his bedroom door. Glancing back, she catches the corner of his face, and an unexplainable grief comes over her as the door closes.

Shaking it off as just constant disappointment, Mira buttons her coat, accepting the fact long ago that he will never change.

Billy hearing the garage door open and his mom's car pulling away from the house, whispers. "At last!" Finally he's alone. Shivering, he notices a flock of goose bumps breaking out across his body.

Sweeping into the living room, Billy flings himself onto the couch, never feeling the razor sharp stiletto pierce the back of his skull and slide into his brain, or see the sleek black silhouette slither out the door.

❄ ❄ ❄

Sheriff Anderson is freezing. Why in the sand-hill did he volunteer to take Norris, Mrs. Jakes bloodhound, to the vet?

He can't believe this bag of bones is still breathing. Gagging from the, rot blending with dog breath smells, Jon rolls down the window and leans his head out. Norris, drooling in the back seat tries to nudge in next to Jon's head, but the sheriff pushes him back.

"Norris, sit down." Jon orders. The aging hound does as he's told, but first lets out a disgruntled deaf ringing howl. Trying to calm the canine, Jon reaches his hand back, and pets Norris' snout. "Everything's okay, boy, we'll be there soon enough. Nothing to be afraid of."

Slowing the cruiser down to let Mira Mendelson pull out of her driveway, Norris begins twirling around in circles, scratching at the windows, bounding at the door.

"It's okay, Norris, calm down." Jon has no idea what's gotten into the dog.

He's out of control.

Turning toward the back, Jon grabs the collar and yanks him down on the seat.

"You've been to the vet before, what's the big deal."

Waving to Mira as she drives away, Jon thinks he sees something odd by the living room bay window, but then attributes it to the morning shadows. He continues to slowly drive down the ice coated road.

At last, Norris calms down, and Jon figures he must've seen a squirrel, or some kind of animal that made him so crazy. Dogs are funny that way, they can sense things humans can't, Sheriff Anderson tells himself, pulling into the parking lot of the Mongoose Falls Veterinary Clinic.

✸ ✸ ✸

Waking up, Jimmy fumbles for the pack of Camels laying on the night stand. His head is pounding, and his stomach gurgles like Lake Chernobyl, but that's not going to keep him from smoking. Shaking one out of the pack, he lights the cigarette with a Zippo.

Inhaling deeply, he feels the sting of the tobacco tickle his lungs, and leaning over to cough, spits into the waste basket. Laying back down, he takes another drag, blowing the blue smoke out in tiny ringlets.

Surveying the clothes spewed room, with scattered crushed beer cans lining the chest of drawers, Jimmy realizes that his homosexual DNA is a little defunct. He isn't a clean queen, or a fashion fairy like the stereotypical gay guy.

Maybe it's the influence of living in a small town, and having to act like a butch and not a bitch. People pretending they understand, but not really. They smile at him on the streets, but once they think they're out of ear shot, Jimmy hears the snide whispers and cynical giggles coming from his so-called-neighbors.

His friends are few, Candy Jane really *is* the only one. Of course, he has drinking buddies he went to high school with, but even they give him the side-eye wondering when he'll make a move on them. A few, hopefully wanting an advance.

"That's life." He mumbles to himself, stubbing out his cigarette in the over flowing ashtray on the floor. Climbing out of bed, shivers race through him, as the chill of the night floats in his room like a silver vapor. He now wishes he had turned on the floor board heaters before going to bed, forgoing the inevitable high gas bill.

Noticing how late it is, Jimmy rushes to the television and turns it on. He almost forgot about his favorite soap opera, *All My Children*. He's been a fan for almost a quarter of a century now, since the daytime drama first aired. He considers himself a distant relative to the clan of Pine Valley, enduring countless tragedies, frequent happy times, and constant ill-advised love affairs. Erica, Palmer, Ruth and Joe, have helped Jimmy sustain more than a few bad times in his day.

Their dramas make his life seem rather trivial.

Pondering Candy's problem, Jimmy knows the only smart thing she can do is get rid of Billy. He's a loser, always has been, and Candy deserves better than that. Plus, he's a toad. That red thinning hair, and all of those freckles. Ick!

Suddenly, out of the blue, Sheriff Anderson pops into Jimmy's thoughts. Now, there's a hunk. His solid sharp features, outlined by his dark curly hair. He never seems to age, and Jimmy feels he's one of the most beautiful men in town.

Trouncing over to the window, Jimmy whips open the curtains like a bad actor booed off stage. "Whoa!" He exclaims. This has to be the biggest snow fall all year, he surmises, instinctually wanting to go pounce into the drifts. But his hung over stomach, somersaults at the idea.

He needs a beer.

Going to the fridge, he opens the door and grabs a cold

one. Twisting the top off, he downs half the pale ale, and then burps out loud. Finishing the rest in one gulp, he immediately feels better, and pours himself a cup of coffee. The machine is on a timer, so the brew is ready for him when he wakes up.

Oh, the benefits of modern technology, he chuckles, sitting down in front of the Magnavox. Taking a sip of coffee, he burns the tip of his tongue. Cursing under his breath, Jimmy hopes it doesn't blister; he has a hot date after work tonight, and he doesn't want anything to spoil it. Jimmy hasn't told this to anyone, but he believes he's falling in love.

Candy Jane plugs in the iron, annoyed at the efficiency of the Mongoose Falls Public Works Department. They've already cleared off all the streets, so life is back to normal. Candy can't believe it, she has to go to work.

Jiggling the frayed extension cord, she hears the faint flicker of sparks as the red light blinks slightly. Steam hisses from the dirty plate. Maybe it's about time she invests in a new iron.

Waving her hand close to the griddle, she feels heat ooze out. Bending over, Candy rummages through her clean laundry, forever piled in her wicker clothes basket. Dragging out a wrinkled white shirt, she looks at it closely. Food stains dot the yellowing fabric. Candy Jane hates wearing white at work, she usually smears the blouse with something even before she puts it on.

Dismayed, Candy considers her job, and sneers at the thought of the customers. Most of them are locals, but during the summer, tourists occupy the tables, and they are getting ruder every year. Just last month Candy had a problem with a guy who was drunk and only left her ten dollars on a hundred dollar check.

"That's the business." She whispers to herself.

After creasing the sleeves, she presses the collar, noticing that it's already two-thirty. She's supposed to be at Billy's by three. There's no way she'll make it there before three-fifteen.

Contemplating the idea of just calling him to say she can't make it because she's running late, Candy knows deep down it's just another excuse to avoid the inevitable. She has to get this over with. She'll say she needs some time to herself, take a little breather, get some space. Hopefully he won't be a cry baby, and accept the situation for what it is.

Candy has her doubts.

Dressing, Candy slips into the kitchen, and opening a cupboard, pulls down a can of cat food. Peeling the tin lid back, she hears it burp, and watches as Amelia comes running into the kitchen, excited about this rare treat.

Deep in her thoughts, Candy jumps at the ringing phone. Reaching up, she yanks the receiver off the hook. She's one of the few people left in Mongoose Falls who still owns a land-line. Most of the residents opting for cell phones, carrying them around like they're the most important people in the world.

"Hello!"

Jimmy's voice brings Candy back to the moment. "Jimmy, hey, I was just walking out the door. What do you want?"

"Why are you leaving so early."

"I'm stopping by Billy's before I go to work."

"Are you going to break up with him?" Jimmy snickers.

"I'm going to tell him I need a little free time, and then see what happens." Candy sneezes. "So I need to go."

"Oh, darn, I'm wondering if you can pick me up."

"What happened to your truck?"

"I had to give it back."

"You know Billy lives clear across town, right?"

"Yeah, I know. Maybe you should come get me now, and I can go with you. Show some moral support."

"I don't think so. I don't have time to pick you up, so find someone else, okay?" That's the last thing she needs, for Jimmy to be tagging along. Billy can't stand him, calls him Mallow Cup.

"Okay, but you owe me one. I'll see you at work."

"I don't owe you crap. Bye."

Hanging up the phone, Candy throws her coat on, and grabs the open box of Fruit Loops off the counter. Stuffing them in her pocket, she figures she might get hungry later.

❋　❋　❋

Jimmy Prescott hangs up the phone, a little put off by how curt Candy's being. "Fine, then." He whips his head back and pulls a cigarette out of the almost empty pack. He'll have to remember to stop and buy more.

He lied about the truck, it's still parked in the driveway. He didn't want to drive because his first beer turned into a six pack. He feels fine now, but he knows he'll continue to drink throughout the night, and eventually need a ride home anyway, why not just plan ahead.

A thin coating of clammy sweat sizzles Jimmy's skin, so he decides on a quick shower before he leaves. Plus, it might sober him up a little bit, and get rid of the booze smell. Smiling as he steps into the steaming shower, Jimmy prays Candy Jane will hold fast to her guns this time, and finally dump Billy Mendelson.

Candy Jane is late, really late. She knows Billy's going to give her hell for it, too. What does it matter? She's going to break up with him anyway. Wrapping a scarf around her neck and zipping up her coat, Candy feels invincible in her puffy orange parka. Nothing can touch her; no sleet, no snow, no furious man.

Scanning the living room for the kitty, Candy doesn't see her, and figures the feline must be in her new favorite spot, probably having dessert at the, *Y*! "See you later, Amelia." Candy shouts.

Reaching for the door knob, and taking a deep breath, Candy braces herself as she steps outside. Blowing snow slaps her in the face, as she whimpers under the stinging winter bite. It's colder today than yesterday, now that the sky has opened up, letting the heat escape. Trudging through the white powder, Candy makes it to her car, and slides inside. It's like sitting in an ice cube.

Turning the key, she listens as the car sputters to life, then dies. Counting to ten, she tries again, this time the motor roars in disapproval. Candy keeps her foot on the accelerator, revving the engine.

Feeling the idle click, Candy grabs the plastic red scraper from the back seat, dreading the chore of chipping the ice off the windows. Maybe she should move to Florida where she wouldn't have to deal with this. Leave right now, grab the cat and take off, not call anyone until she gets there. What's wrong with running away from your problems?

Giggling to herself, Candy Jane finishes and jumps back into the car where it's a little warmer. Wiping the fog off her watch, she sees that it is ten after three. "Oh, damn," Candy curses, she'll barely have time to say hi.

Grinding the shift into gear, she slips down the drive, and fishtails onto the plowed street. Cars line the sides, buried by the mounds of piled snow. Candy's thankful for her driveway, and the teen-age boy who's on contract to shovel her walk for the winter. She pays him a lot, but it's worth it.

Because of the clear and empty roads, Candy finds herself pulling up in front of Billy's sooner than she expects. Sitting for a moment, she reaches into her pocket, fumbling for the Fruit Loops. Tossing some in her mouth, Candy studies the Mendelson's house. It looks rather dark and eerie for some reason. Even though the day is bright and sunny with a few clouds sprinkled about, a shadow casts darkness around the relic.

Candy sloshes up the pathway, knowing Mrs. Mendelson has shoveled the walk. Her lazy son doesn't even know how to use a shovel. As she steps onto the porch, she notices how quiet the place is. Usually the television is blaring, or Billy's rocking out to Ted Nugent.

Maybe he's taking a nap, Candy thinks, as she raps three times on the door.

Sheriff Jon Anderson sits down in his hard-back-wooden-chair and lifts his feet up onto the desk. The office is empty, and the only sounds are the comforting creaks of the old Town Hall building. He's finally warmed up after being outside all day, and now all he wants to do is sit back and relax for a few minutes.

Jon regards the weather report he has just received over the line. Another storm is heading their way, as the winds whirl ferociously, and the skies grow dark. He dismissed all of his deputies early, and figuring there's nothing to rush home to, decided to stay and get some much needed work done.

For a while now, Jon's been feeling like he's in the way when he's home. Whenever he walks into a room where Carol is, she sighs in disappointment, as though he's disturbing her. Not long ago, when he'd enter, she'd jump into his arms. My how things have changed.

Lacing his hands behind his head, Jon leans back and closes his eyes. He doesn't know how much longer he can take it. He has his desires, and even though he's a very patient man, he *is* a man, and he needs release. He's beginning to understand why married men start having affairs after the sex stops.

It's not as though there's much choice here in Mongoose Falls. The only woman he'd even be interested in, would be Candy Jane Cane. Jon's always been a little bit attracted to her. He thinks she's cute.

Shaking his head, Jon's thoughts of infidelity surprise him. He loves Carol, and will never do anything to hurt her. Isn't that what marriage and commitment is all about, making sacrifices for the relationships happiness?

Shifting in his chair, Jon sees a beam of light float across the wall. Who would be out with a storm approaching? Walking over to the window, he watches as Candy Jane's car disappears around the corner. Wonder where she's going, Jon scratches his chin, remembering Mira's house is in that direction.

He has no idea what Candy sees in Billy Mendelson.

As the office grows dimmer, Jon turns on a lamp next to the file cabinet. The room glows in a soft yellow. Maybe he should start heading home before the blizzard really hits, he reckons, kind of wishing he could just stay here all night, but knows Carol will have a fit.

Snow twisters race down the street as Jon watches in awe. He's lived here his whole life, and is still amazed at the raw, and unforgiving power of Mother Nature. There's a sense of isolation, a drawing back into a time of nothingness.

The static from the radio snaps Jon back to the here and now, and figuring it's going to be a slow night in this hick town, he decides to go home. Maybe he'll open a bottle of wine, make a nice roaring fire, and try to ease his wife back into their bed.

Straightening a few papers on his desk, he turns off the light and heads into the blistering cold evening.

3

Candy Jane stands at the door shivering, waiting for Billy to let her in. A gust of wind whips her hat off, and glancing behind her, notices the snow is beginning to fall again. Is there another Northerner heading their way?

Looking up at the house, she finds it odd that there's not a single light on. Knocking again, Candy yelps. "Come on Billy, open up, this isn't funny, it's cold out here." She wants to make this quick, explain to him that it's not the end, just a little vacation of sorts. Ringing the bell, Candy grabs the knob and twists, the door creaks open.

"This is weird," Candy whispers to herself, as she peeks into the house. Mira's a stickler about keeping the doors locked, even when they're home. She always maintains that it's harder to get into a locked house than an unlocked one. Candy figures something must have happened in the past to Mrs. Mendelson.

The smell of greasy mothballs floats like a fog, and for a second Candy's reminded of her grandmother. Silence wraps around her, as the hairs on the back of her neck stand on end.

"Billy, you here?"

Sneaking to the staircase, Candy listens at the landing, but hears nothing. Maybe he left, she thinks, a little relieved at the idea. This way she can just deal with him tomorrow. Always do the things you can do now, later, is Candy's mantra.

Tossing some Fruit Loops into her mouth, Candy Jane enters the kitchen, and sees the breakfast dishes still on the table. Mira must have left before Billy finished. Turning into the living room, she looks toward the couch and sees Billy laying there motionless. Something seems odd about him, Candy chills, easing closer to the body.

Suddenly, she realizes he's not breathing. Rushing over to him, she touches his arm and feels it stiff and cold. A stream of dried blood lines his chin.

"Billy?" Candy jiggles him, his body holds no life.

She needs to get help. Reaching for the phone, she doesn't notice the falling Fruit Loops tumbling from her pocket. Punching in 911, Candy Jane holds the receiver to her ear. The line buzzes empty. Not seeing the unplugged cord, Candy believes there's no connection because of the weather. Now, more than ever, she wishes she owned a cell phone.

Frantically, Candy wonders if Billy had a heart attack, but why would there be blood trickling out of his mouth?

There's no sign of a struggle, so maybe he fell somehow and snapped his neck. What if he was killed and the murderer is still in the house?

Panic grips Candy Cane, like a bout of gout. Scared, she knows she needs to find Sheriff Anderson, and tries to recall where the closest pay phone is. She begins to regret not giving Jimmy a ride. Inching herself back to the vestibule, Candy tries not to make any of the floor boards creak.

Dashing out the door, she remembers Mrs. Mendelson and wonders where she is, or is her body laying elsewhere in the house? Sliding to her car, Candy jumps in and turns the ignition. The still warm motor starts right up. Peeling away, she doesn't look back.

Driving toward town on the slick streets, Candy turns her wipers on as the snow starts sleeting more fiercely. The most sensible thing she can do is go to the sheriff's office. She noticed a cruiser parked in front of the building when she drove by earlier. Hopefully, somebody's still there.

Tears begin to stream down Candy's face as she thinks about Billy. She's convinced herself that he's been murdered, and wonders, if she had arrived on time, could she have prevented this from happening?

Shivers cross her body as Candy Jane speeds down Main Street, whip-lashing into the Town Hall parking lot. Sliding sideways, she almost knocks over a handy-capped sign. The only thing saving her from plowing into the red brick building is the curb.

Opening her door, she steps out, her coat flailing in the winds, the cold of no factor to her right now. Running up the steps to the closed front doors, Candy yanks the oblong handle, and almost falls back as her fingers slip from the metal. She tries again, it's locked.

Noticing a piece of paper taped to the window, she leans closer and reads. *"Gone home, storms coming in. For any emergencies call #531-1344. Sheriff Anderson."*

Twirling around, she tries to spot something open. Every door is dark. The town has closed up for the night, and it's barely four. What's she going to do? Her most logical idea is to go to Sven's. She's positive Toth has the restaurant open, and she can call Sheriff Anderson from there.

Running back to her car, Candy catches a patch of ice. Her feet slip out from beneath her as she flies up into the air, landing directly on her lower back. "Oh, crap," she groans, sitting up on the frozen cement. Standing, she limps to the car, thankful it's still nice and warm. This is turning into a nightmare, she reflects, jamming the stick into gear and heading east toward Route 9.

Crawling along the deserted highway, Candy knows the last thing she wants to do is fly into a snow bank. The gusts groan, as the oaks howl like widowed women, and the bent over evergreens, remind her of tired athletes. Candy catches herself feeling a little creeped out and scared.

Big flat flakes begin to fall more steadily, and Candy knows that if she goes to Sven's, and the blizzard gets really bad, she might be stuck there. But she can always call Bill...

Remembering he's dead, she starts crying all over again. This time the tears are as thick and wet as the snow outside.

❋ ❋ ❋

"Thank golly," Sheriff Anderson mumbles, as he tapes the note to the door. Jon doesn't see any sense in sticking around the office, when he can be safe and sound at home. He's sure nothing is going to happen this evening. You'd have to be crazy roaming outside tonight.

Opting for the motorized sled, Jon jumps on the ski-doo, knowing it'll get him where he wants to be a lot faster. Plus, he loves riding the Yamaha. Racing across the country side, he feels like a kid again. The majestic beauty of the silver-slick-slopes always mesmerizes him. His primeval instincts roar alive in the freshness of the raw beauty.

Turning off of the shortcut and onto his street, Jon sees Mira getting out of her car, and decides to stop and say, hi. He slows a few feet away from her, and waves.

"Evening, Mira."

She looks toward him. "Jon, that you?"

"Yeah, I'm just heading home and figured I'd stop and see how you're holding out in this weather."

"As well as can be expected. I'm just getting back from Mrs. Abernathy's. Me and Carol cleaned out her attic, I tell you, talk about a packrat." Mira giggles. "We had a good time, though."

"You said, Carol?"

"Yeah."

"Oh!" Jon's a little put off because he knew nothing about it.

Noticing his dismay, Mira chimes in. "It was a last minute thing. I didn't realize I needed help until I got there, and Carol was kind enough to come over and give me a hand." Mira pauses for a moment. "She really is a dear." Another hesitation. "Why, is there a problem?"

"No, should there be? Carol can do as she pleases." Jon thinks his voice sounds a little too crisp. Lowering his head, he sees red tail lights speeding toward town.

"Would you like to come in for a cup of cocoa, Jon?"

Regretting that he stopped, he replies. "No, I don't think so, Mira. Carol's waiting for me at home, so I'd better get going. Maybe another time."

"Well, hang on a minute. Carol wants a quart of my apricot jam. I can save her a trip and just give it to you. I'll be right out."

Before Jon has a chance to protest, Mira's heading toward the house. Tightening his gloves around his wrist, trying to bide time, he glances up when he sees Mira rush out the door screaming.

"Jon, Jon, come quick, it's Billy. Something's wrong with him."

Now he really wishes he would have kept on going. Flicking the ski-doo off, he bounds up the sidewalk, and reaches a whimpering Mira.

"Hurry Jon, I can't wake him. He's in the living room."

"Mira, take it easy. Wait here and I'll go have a look." Side-stepping past her and into the house, he feels Mira on his heels. Turning around, Jon places his hands on her shoulders. "Let me check this out first, okay?"

"I suppose." Mira's eyes fill with fear.

Sheriff Jon Anderson has only seen one dead body in his whole life, and that was at his grandma's funeral. He has never seen a corpse before they were drained and stitched up.

He can't focus at first. Sniffing the room, he smells Billy's waste. Gagging, Jon covers his face with his gloved hand, and moves closer to the body. Bending over Billy, he touches his neck for a pulse, but his veins lay still.

Leaning closer, Jon notices a small trickle of red spreading out from under Billy's head. Being careful, he rolls him over on his side, and studies the back of his neck. A small puncture hole at the base of his skull is dried with blood.

"Murdered?" Jon whispers, feeling a little woozy. He reaches out for the couch and steadies himself. "Who would do something like this?"

"Sheriff, Sheriff Anderson." He hears Mira's voice approaching. "Is Billy all right? Is hee…" Coming around the corner, she sees Jon holding Billy's stiffening body on his side. "Oh, my gosh!" Mira runs over to her son. "Billy, oh no, Billy, this isn't happening."

Almost knocking Jon over, Mira bundles her son's dead body in her arms and starts sobbing.

Dazed, Mira raises her hand and sees red staining her fingers. It doesn't take her long to realize it's her son's blood. Screaming, she swings her fist at Jon. He ducks, barely being missed by the blow.

"Someone killed him?"

"We don't know that for sure." Jon tries to ward off the

pounding jabs.

Finally gaining control over her flailing fists, Jon reassures. "Mira, we'll get to the bottom of this, but right now, you need to calm down."

The shattered mother gazes up at Jon, her eyes sunken, and lightly says. "Who would do a thing like this? Billy never hurt anyone in his life. Sure, he's lazy and doesn't like to work, but he has a good heart. I don't understand." Her face sinks into her hands and Mira begins bawling again.

Fumbling inside the pocket of his parka, Jon pulls out his cell phone, speed dialing his first deputy Mark Pickens. Listening to the ring, Jon figures the murder weapon has to be something like a razor sharp stiletto that can pierce the brain so precise. But where is the stealth dagger?

"Hallow."

"Mark, hey Mark, it's Jon."

"Jon, what up?"

"I need you at the Mendelson's house right away, but first find Gear. Tell him to go to the office and wait for my instructions"

"Where are you?"

Jon shakes his head. Mark's not the brightest color in the box, but he's loyal, and does a good job, and to Jon, those are two worthy characteristics.

"I'm at Mira Mendelson's house. Now hurry."

"Aren't you gonna tell me what happened?"

"I'll fill you in when you get here." Jon is about to hang up when her remembers. "Hey, tell Gear to contact the State Police, let them know we have an emergency." He pauses.

"Oh, and Mark," a sudden blankness fills the line. The cell towers must be blocked by the snow.

Snapping the phone closed, Jon stands there for a moment, trying to process the events of the last fifteen minutes. He has to follow protocol, otherwise it might come back to haunt him later. The first thing he needs to do is secure the crime scene, which means getting Mira out of there.

Returning to the living room, Jon notices Mira is still sitting next to Billy, combing his thin red hair back with her hand. That's not good, Jon thinks to himself, going over to her and resting his hands on her shoulders.

"Mira, I need you to come with me. I have to tape off this area, and you really shouldn't be touching anything."

The stricken woman stares blankly at him. "I have no one now, Jon. My whole family is gone. Do you know what that feels like?"

Trying to raise her, Jon replies. "No, Mira I don't, but I do know that with time, things will get easier. You've been there before, you know." As soon as he speaks those words, he regrets them. "Oh, golly, I'm sorry, I really didn't mean to say that. Sometimes, I'm just an idiot." His apology sounding clumsy.

Leading her away from the body, Jon escorts Mira to the kitchen and eases her into a chair. "Just stay put for now. Mark's going to be here in a minute, and he'll make you some tea. I need to go investigate the area. So, will you be okay by yourself for a little while?"

"Yes, Jon." A lobotomized tone spills from her lips.

Anxious to start his search, Jon trounces down the hall.

As he's about to enter the living room, he steps on something crunchy. Glancing down, he sees a few scattered Fruit Loops sprinkled on the floor. Snapping a pair of rubber gloves out of his pocket, Jon pulls them on. The tightness yanks at his hairy hands. Picking a few sugar ringlets up, he drops them into a plastic evidence bag, and wonders where the cereal bowl is. Billy is still donned in his pajamas, so Jon figures he must have been eating breakfast when he was stabbed.

"Sheriff Jon, where are you?"

His young deputy enters the room, and without thinking yelps. "Geeze, it smells in here. Who took a shit?" His young wife, Delores, who is glued to his arm, suddenly releases him and runs out, choking.

"What's Delores doing here, Mark? You know better." Jon squats down, searching for more cereal.

"I thought she might be able to help somehow."

Mark and Delores Pickens are newlyweds, and seldom, since being married three months ago, do you ever see them apart.

"Well, since she's here, tell her to go keep Mira company in the kitchen. Maybe help her with some tea or coffee, whatever. Just keep her out of the way." Feeling slightly agitated, Jon snips at Mark.

"Fine, fine, you don't have to get your panties in a wad, gosh." Mark disappears and then returns quickly. "Wow! This is so cool Jon, a real murder."

"Focus, Mark, this is no joke."

Inching closer to the corpse, the six foot man seems more

like a child easing up to a opened-creaking-closet after a nightmare.

"Hurry up, Mark, we don't have all night. This is valuable time we're wasting."

"How'd he die, Jon" Adapting to the situation, Mark begins to sound all Dragnet like. "Is it a break-in, a fight, did he commit suicide?"

"I'm not sure yet." For some reason Jon's nerves are raw. "I just know he's dead, and we need to secure this area before help gets here."

"The State Police are coming?" A squealing excitement laces Mark's voice.

"Are you ever gonna grow up?"

"What'da mean?"

"Oh, nothing!" Jon waves a hand at him. "Did you bring the kit in?"

"Ohhh, no, it's in the car."

"Well, you better go get it, then tape this room off and start dusting for fingerprints."

"It's freezing out there."

"That's what you get for not bringing it in to begin with, now go, Mark." Jon's getting perturbed.

Deputy Pickens whirls his fullback sized body around, and heads out the door. "This isn't very much fun for being our first murder." He slams the door behind him, rattling the chandelier in the foyer.

Shaking his head, Jon senses it's going to be a long night.

❄ ❄ ❄

The day dims at the *Mongoose Falls Bar and Billiards*, as Jimmy picks up his glass and downs the chilled liquor. He glances at his watch. Three-fifty-five, the digital face winks at him. He needs to cruise, vetoing the idea of having one last drink.

Staring out the window, Jimmy is hypnotized as the snow continues to pile up. Maybe he should just call in, see if they really need him. They certainly aren't going to be busy. Anybody in their right mind will be staying put tonight, including his less-than-hot date.

Sliding thirty-five cents off the bar, Jimmy sashays toward the back where the bathrooms and phones are. Adjusting his gate, he stiffens and lumbers past the Neanderthals hovering around the pool tables, who grunt, "faggot."

Experience has taught Jimmy not to react, as he ignores the hate filled slur. He's in no mood to get his ass kicked.

Darting into the dimness, he straddles the blue and silver pay phone, and drops the coins into the slot. Hearing a shallow clunk, and then a dial tone, his pointy finger punches in seven numbers, ringing once before it's answered.

"Sven's All You Can Eat Smorgasbord."

"Patricia, is that you?"

"Yes, is this Jimmy." She always sounds so formal.

"Yeah, hey I'm just calling…"

She cut him off mid-sentence. "Are you still at home?"

"Yeah." Lying.

"Well stay there." Knowing he's in a bar by the background noises. "We're closing. Another doozer is heading our way, and Sven says to shut her down, totally against

Toth's wishes."

"That's great!"

"Uh-huh, I'm just about out the door myself."

Jimmy listens as Patricia inhales a cigarette and wishes he had one with him. "Is Candy Jane there?"

"Nope, I haven't seen her."

"Oh, really?"

"Why, is she supposed to be?"

"I just figured she'd be there by now. She was stopping by Billy's and then heading to work. She probably lost track of time."

"Yes, probably."

Jimmy can tell Patricia wants to get off the line, so he concludes. "If she comes in, tell her to call me at home."

"I will. Night Jimmy."

"Good-bye, Patricia. Careful driving home."

"Okay."

The Swiss hangs up the phone, and Jimmy remains statuesque for a moment deciding what to do next. Dancing a little jig on the way back to his seat, he notices a fresh drink on the bar. Sitting down, and wondering who the secret admirer is, Chuck the bartender appears and says.

"Hey Jimmy, this one's on me. But then I'm closing up for the night before the roads get any worse."

"That's fine, Chuck. Thanks." He raises his glass and nods. "I need to head out, too. I'm still not recovered from yesterdays storm."

"Me either, and they say this one is really packing a punch." Chuck swings his fist through the air.

Relighting a half smoked cigarette crunched in the ashtray, Jimmy glances around the almost empty bar, and waves Chuck over with his fingers. Leaning in close, he slurs. "Hey, do ya think you can sell me a fifth of Jack. I'll pay you big for it."

"I'm not supposed to Jimmy, you know the rules, I could lose my license.

"No one will ever know. Just stash it in the trash, and then when you dump the bags, I'll be there to dig it out."

"I don't know, Jimmy."

"Ah, come on." Laying a fifty on the bar, Jimmy continues to plead. "Here, this should take care of my tab, and the rest is for you."

Chuck glances up at the ceiling, thinking how slow it's been lately, and how that little bit of cash will sure come in handy. He can just write it off as breakage. "Oh, all right, but just this one time."

Sliding another twenty across the oak bar, Jimmy asks. "And can you throw a six pack of Bud in there, too?" Smiling, he watches as Chuck shuffles away, shaking his head while stuffing the money into his pocket.

Downing the rest of his drink, Jimmy makes a quick pit stop, and then heads out the door just as the proprietor reappears. "Good night, Chuck."

"Night, Jimmy. Be careful out there." He winks at Jimmy, which seems unnatural.

Rushing around to the back, he finds the bag of booze stuffed on top of the heap. The brown paper has already started to get wet from the snow, so Jimmy carefully lifts it and holds the package to his chest like a new born.

Being extra cautious, Jimmy shuffles slowly to his car, and jumps in. Starting the cold vehicle, he waits for a moment before stepping outside to clear his windows. Opening the bag sitting next to him, he's disappointed to see that Chuck has given him aluminums instead of bottles. Jimmy hates drinking out of a can, he thinks it's too butch.

"Oh, well," he says, ripping one from the plastic holder and popping it open. White foam fizzles to the top, and Jimmy sucks it off. Stepping out of the truck, he clears the windows quickly, leaving patches of snow everywhere. The air is bitter cold; it's like breathing inside of an ice cube. Jimmy feels his jewels recede.

Shivering, he slides behind the steering wheel, and shoves the gear into first. Taking a long swig off of his beer, he carefully pulls out. No sense in being reckless, he cautions, as he crawls along the deserted road.

❋   ❋   ❋

Candy Jane can barely see the sign on the pole which reads, *Sven's Smorgasbord,* as driving snow pelts harder against her windshield, making the wipers squeal in agony. Darkness piles up around her as Candy loses sight of the red tail lights that were up ahead.

Turning into the empty lot circling around to the door, she notices the building is dark and still, and the security gate is locked. What is she going to do now?

A pounding on the hood startles her, and looking to her

left, sees Toth's face, blurred and distorted. He gestures for her to roll down her window.

"What are you doing, scaring me like that?" She cackles at him.

"I didn't mean too." Hectors tone seems different. "Listen, we've been trying to get hold of you. We're closing for the night." He glances at his watch. "You would've been late, anyway." He's trying to be funny, it's not working.

"Bite me, Toth." Seeing his face pout, Candy Jane feels a little sorry for him. "I'm only joking, Hector. I'm just a little on edge." She starts to roll up her window, but Toth puts his hand on it.

"Where you going?"

"I need to find a phone."

Hector's heart skips a beat. "I have one at my house, and it's just down the road."

"Can't you just open the restaurant, so I can use the one in there."

"The lines are down?" Lying.

"Well, if they're down here, then they must be down at your house."

"I have a cell phone."

"Really? I never see you with it."

"I keep it at home. Nobody ever calls me, so I really don't use it, except for emergencies."

Candy's not sure if Toth is trying to play on her sympathies, or not.

Contemplating the situation, and going against her instincts, she opts to go with Toth. She'll call Sheriff Anderson, and then get the hell outta there, no matter how bad the weather gets. She'd rather be stranded in a blizzard, than be stuck at Hector's.

"Okay, but let's make it fast."

"Great!" He seems to be a little more excited than necessary, Candy notices. "Why don't you go park, and I'll drive."

"No, I think I'll take my car." Candy begins to feel a little uncomfortable.

"There's no need to take two cars, I'll bring you back when you're finished."

"I wouldn't feel right, you having to come back out in this mess."

"It's no problem, Candy Jane."

"I'll just follow you." Toth's starting to give her the hee-bie-jeebies.

"Okay, have it your way." He steps back, and strolls to his gray Suburban, parked behind Candy Jane. Turning around before getting in, he sneers. "Just don't lose me." He excels out of the driveway, spinning a figure-eight in the road.

"Jerk!" Candy hisses, wishing it would have been anyone but Toth helping her. She speeds up to catch him.

There has only been one other time she's been to his house, and that was for a party, which turned out to be a bust. Candy, having nothing better to do, shows up. And sad to say, was the only one. It was unbearable, but they grudged it out for an hour, making small talk and drinking way too many beers.

Toth's anger and disappointment began to show, fueled by the no-shows. In a way, Candy Jane felt bad for him, she could tell he was really looking forward to the gathering.

Right now though, she's feeling no sympathy as he peels through the streets, like a Greyhound after a rabbit, forcing Candy Jane to drive faster than she wants to. Trying to locate a landmark of some sort, Candy recognizes nothing, as the sleek snow shimmies her car.

Watching him turn left and then disappear, Candy experiences a sense of timelessness, like she's driving in the middle of a snowball. Retrieving her senses, she spots Toth's lights stopping up ahead in his driveway.

Wheeling in next to his vehicle, she tries to stop but skids, halting just inches from the garage door. Shaking her head, and wishing she were dead, Candy Jane gets out of the car and hears Toth screaming from his porch.

"Hey, park in the street."

Candy Jane glances at the mountains of snow lining the curbs. "You're crazy. No one will be able to get through. "Don't worry, I'm not going to be here for long."

Stomping to the door, she yanks it open and steps in. A stale cigar scent greets her, and Candy tries not to gag. "Maybe we should keep the door open for a little while. Let some fresh air in."

Toth comes up from behind her, and closes it forcefully. "Don't be an idiot, it's cold outside."

Candy moves away from him. "You know Hector, maybe this isn't such a good idea." She reaches for the handle.

"No, wait, Candy Jane. I'm sorry. I guess I'm just a little riled because we closed." He grunts. "Personally, I think we should've stayed open.""Toth, no one's going out tonight. You need to take the well being of the crew into consideration, too."

"You made it in."

"Hurrah for me!" Candy says in her head, wishing she'd stayed on the couch. "Well, who's the stupid one?"

"You're not stupid, Candy Jane." Toth whispers.

"What?"

"Oh, I said the phone is in the corner." He points. "I'm going to grab myself a beer. Want one?"

Yes, she did, but she wasn't going to. "No, thanks. I need to make this quick."

"Who you calling?"

"That's really none of your business." Walking over to the hula-woman shaped phone, Candy removes the receiver from its green-patched-port. What a freak, she thinks, where'd he ever get a cell like this? Probably custom made, Candy concludes, as she punches in 911, and lifting the figurine to her ear, flinches as the plastic breasts pokes her cheek.

Silence!

Candy redials, but still, nothing. "Dagnabit," she yells, slamming the thatch-skirted girl back into her pond of grass. "Toth, your phone is dead."

"No, it's not, you just don't know how to use it." He appears out of the darkened kitchen holding two beers, and extends one to her.

❀   ❀   ❀

"I told you I didn't want one." She grabs it instinctually.

"Just sit down and relax, honey, we'll figure something out."

"Honey?" Her mind screams. Why is he calling her, "Honey?"

He moseys closer to her, and tries to touch her arm, but she steps back. "What you need to do is calm down, Candy Jane."

"Don't tell me how I should be." Candy's irritability rising to the surface. She pauses for a moment, gathering herself. "Listen, Toth, I really need to get to a phone, so I'm gonna head out." Setting her untouched beer on the messy coffee table. "Thanks anyway, Hector. I appreciate your help."

"You know, it's getting pretty dangerous out there. Maybe you should just spend the night, and then I can take you home in the morning."

"Is he joking?" Candy cries inside. "Don't be ridicules, Hector. We've both driven in worse conditions." But to be honest, Candy Jane can't recall a storm as bad as this one in all her years of living in Mongoose Falls, which is all her life.

Suddenly, a cramp shoots through her ovaries and Candy knows that all-too-familiar jolt. "I just need to use your bathroom before I leave, okay?"

"Yeah, sure. You all right?" Toth seeing her face cringe.

"You don't look so good."

"I'm fine, I just have to pee." Candy does a quick mental inventory of the contents of her bag, and prays she has a tampon if what she thinks is happening, is.

What timing!

The bath is filthy, gross, a gray tinge reflects from the mirror. Locking the door, Candy unzips her slacks, and much to her relief sees her period pulled a false alarm. Realizing she really does have to pee, she side-eyes the toilet, and decides she'd rather freeze doing it outside, than touch anything in this bacteria basin.

What a mistake coming here. He probably knew all along that his phone was dead, and lured her to his house under false pretenses. It doesn't surprise her. Lately, Candy Jane has begun to sense that Toth might have a crush on her, or more.

Entering the kitchen, Candy finds Toth standing by the sink in nothing but his briefs, bulging from an erection.

Looking away, and feeling mortified, Candy says. "I think I'll get going now," and bolts for the door. She's not fast enough.

Grabbing her arm, Toth flings her against his body, nearly driving himself through her stomach, leaving her breathless. He begins grabbing and squeezing her breasts.

"Damn-it, Hector, get off me." She kicks his shin with her boot. Bending over in pain, Candy pushes him away, and runs out of his grasping clutch.

The ecstasy Toth put into both of their beers is beginning to take effect, as he yells. "Get back here, you slut." Fumbling after her. "You've wanted this for a long time. I'm gonna show you what it's like to be with a real man."

He snags Candy's heel and pulls her down. Hector slithers on top of her, reaching down to undo her pants. She's no match for him. Candy thinks he must be tripping on something, as he tugs at her underwear, giving her a wedgie. She can't believe this is happening to her.

"Oh, Candy, oh, Candy." Toth moans as he tries to insert himself in her, but can't.

Sensing him relax for a instant, Candy swings her leg up, and kicks his hardened manhood, sending him screaming off of her.

"Oh, my gosh! Oh, my gosh, why'd you have to go do that, Candy? I wasn't going to hurt you."

Standing, Candy quickly fastens her jeans, feeling her breasts throb from his groping. "You're an ass-hole, and don't think for a minute that I'm not going to tell people what you did. You tried to rape me, and you're going to pay for this."

Straightening her now wrinkled work shirt, Candy starts for the door. Hector, filled with panic, shoots up and stammers after her, flailing at the empty air. "Please, Candy, can't we just forget about this, I'm sorry. I took something, okay, I'm not myself." Toth seems to sober up.

"You're full of shit, you had this all planned." She thought of the beer he had given her, and knew for sure he'd spiked it. Good thing she didn't take a swig off of it. Reaching for her coat on the chair, Toth jumps in front of her.

"Please, Candy, can't we let this one slide? After all, I

really didn't do anything." He nervously wipes his mouth. "Plus, it's your word against mine."

"Believe me, Toth. They'll know who's telling the truth."

"Come on Candy Jane, this'll ruin me. Isn't there anything I can do."

"You should have thought of that before you attacked me."

Realizing his pleading is useless, Hector begins to lash out. "You're nothing but a dyke, anyway. Hanging out with that fruity fag. I swear..."

Raising his fist, he rushes at her. Ducking his swing, she steps aside, and with all her might, pushes him back. Time slows down, she leaves her body, floating above, watching herself from the corner. The surprise reaction catches Hector off guard as she powerfully knocks him away, his flailing hands unable to catch him as he hits the floor.

Hearing his head crack on the maple wood, as his body goes limp, Candy notices the room becoming all dream-like and hazy, a little chilly, too. Shivers ravage Candy Jane's body, she can't stop shaking.

Inching over to the still torso, Candy keeps thinking of Jackie Kennedy's words; when the unthinkable happens, it changes your life. And right now, Candy Jane knows, the unthinkable just happened.

"Hector, Toth." Candy nudges his arm with her foot. His stiff body is unresponsive. "He's dead," vibrates through her mind as she freezes.

Feeling herself sway, she steps to her right to keep from falling. He tripped, that's what happened, Candy tells herself. And his head didn't hit *that* hard, trying to pacify her nerves. Fear creeps through her, and Candy knows she has to get out of there. She needs to find some help and fast. Maybe it's a heart attack from the drug, or something like that. Possibly a brain aneurysm. Whatever it is, she needs to find someone to assist her.

Zipping up her coat, she thunders out the door. The cold blasts snaps her crazed mind into some distorted reality. She glances back at the house. What if he's not dead? She should have checked for a pulse, or something, but the thought of touching him nauseates her.

Candy's cold-heartedness shocks her.

Too late now!

Turning the ignition key, the cool car sputters. Trying once more, the reluctant motor starts. Candy rubs the dash. "That's the way Ruby, just get me home or to town, and then you can relax for the rest of the night." Great, now she's talking to a car.

Pressing her face as close to the windshield as possible, Candy's barely able to see the road in front of her. Harsh winter gales whip the Red Toyota, shaking and shivering it's small frame. The car backfires, as Candy keeps her foot on the accelerator. Glancing at the gas gauge, she notices the red arrow sits at half, and taking a deep breath crawls back toward town.

Maybe she should go to Jimmy's and tell him what happened. Candy's sure that between the two of them they can figure this out. After all, Jimmy's lived in Minneapolis before, so he has a few more streets smarts than she.

Thinking of Amelia, Candy's glad she over filled the bowl before leaving. Tears pool in her eyes as she wonders if she'll ever see her kitty again.

❋   ❋   ❋

Patricia Moldine ducks down as she watches Candy Jane run from Toth's house. What in the hell is going on, she questions as she begins to open the car door. Suddenly, another pair of headlights recklessly brazes by her, coming to a skidding halt in front of Hector's double-wide.

Cynthia Scotchland rushes out of the jeep, and scampers up to the trailer's coughing frame. Patricia takes a deep breath as she notices Cynthia remove a key from her pocket, and unlock the front door.

Why would she have a key?

Shaking her head, Patricia reconsiders her intentions of surprising Hector with a little wine and dessert, her being the main course. She's never mentioned her feelings for him to anyone, wanting to remain discreet; she is very anti-work-relationships, but in this case, she'll make an exception. There's just something about him. Plus, if she has a boyfriend, she won't seem so out of place in this one-hic-up town. The last thing she wants to do is draw attention to herself.

Deciding to go take a peek at what's happening, Patricia crunches her way to the side window, and peering into the bottom corner, sees Cynthia on top of Hector, riding him like a bucking bronco.

The winds wisp up her wild screams, blending her howls into their own. Slipping and sliding back to her car, Patricia Moldine leans her head against the steering wheel and begins to cry. She'll never find a husband, never have any kids, never change her life from what it was before.

"We'll see about that." Patricia barks, spinning her back tires as they spit out graveled snow. "Nothing has ever gotten in the way of what I want." She snarls, fishtailing away from Toth's.

4

Cynthia Scotchland hates life, everything about it. From her molested filled childhood, to her pathetic adult existence. She can hear the television blaring from the living room, and knows that her parents have just finished dinner and will be retiring in front of the tube until they both pass out into a food coma. They certainly can pack it away, and you can tell by their two hundred and fifty pound bodies.

She detests spending time at their house, but they have a four wheel drive Jeep that she needs to borrow, so she made the sacrifice and endured dinner, but lost her appetite after watching her mom and dad begin eating. There's no returning from that trauma.

Shaking her head, Cynthia knows she has to concentrate on the task at hand; to sneak the vehicle out of the garage without them knowing it. It's important that she sees Hector tonight, and there's nothing that's going to stop her. Cynthia feels like she's jonesin' for some of his lovin'.

Jiggling a mock set of keys in her pocket, she tip-toes out of her childhood bedroom, filled with dark memories, and cranks her head around the corner. Her father lays sprawled in the recliner, like a beached whale, while her mother sits on the couch next to him, head down, chins resting against her heavy bosom, eyes closed, short gasping sighs spitting from her pink juicy lips.

Reaching up to the holder, Cynthia silently exchanges the decoy set with the real keys, figuring neither one of them will be leaving the house tonight, so they'll never notice the difference. Grabbing her coat, she sneaks out of the tin-can-trailer-home and into the frost biting cold.

Quietly opening the garage door, Cynthia surveys the surroundings. Everything's snow covered. It'll be a hell of a time driving in this mess, even with a four wheeler. But she's determined. Climbing into the plastic windowed Jeep, Cynthia wraps her scarf around her hood, tightens on a pair of goggles, and pulls two pair of gloves onto her hands.

Winds nudge the vehicle as she rolls out into the street. Flicking the headlights on, Cynthia watches as the snowflakes sparkle in front of her. It's like a fairyland. Everything is quiet, and a soft echo hums around her. She wonders if this is what being a snowman is like.

Believing she's the only one out tonight, Cynthia is unprepared when a pair of bright beams suddenly appeared out of the fog. She quickly swerves right to avoid the racing car, and feels the jeep scratch against the snow piles heaped on the side of the road.

"Damn-it." She curses, as she tries to avoid crashing into another one. Stopping for a minute, she looks back to see if she knows who it is, but doesn't recognize the car. "Jack-ass."

Easing back onto the street, Cynthia's a little more careful this time, as she rounds a bend and sees Toth's house up ahead. The abode seems kind of different to her, but she can't pin-point what it is. Then, as she inches closer she realizes there aren't any lights on, and thinks maybe the power has gone out in this part of town.

Pulling over, Cynthia turns off the jeep, and grabbing the twelve pack of beer she bought earlier, burrows her way through the deepening snow. Approaching the back, she tries to be quiet. Entering through the unlocked kitchen door, Cynthia notices that the house is cold; there isn't even a fire burning in the wood stove.

At first she thinks maybe he stayed at the restaurant to drink all of Sven's booze, which Hector does quite often, but as she gets closer to the living room, she sees a mound laying in the dining room. She wonders what Toth is doing on the floor, naked?

Bolting over to him, she kneels down next to his body, and licking her lips, examines him. He seems to be alive, very much alive, she smirks, glancing down at his erection. Thinking he's passed out and dreaming of her, Cynthia slips out of her pants and mounts the unconscious man.

"Oh Hector! Oh Hector!" She rides him like a bucking gay rodeo queen, not caring if he's responding. All she knows is that he's never been so hard, and awake or not, she isn't going to miss out on this opportunity.

Rolling her hips around on him, she slides up and down, stimulating herself. She thrust deeply one last time and feels her body shake with spasms. Suddenly, Toth wraps his hands around her hips, and rams hard into her.

"Oh Candy! Oh, Candy Jane."

As Hector orgasms inside of her, she slaps his face, and yanks herself off of him, feeling sick to her stomach. He lifts his head in shock, and seeing it's Cynthia, pushes her away.

"What the hell are you doing?" Toth scurries to the wall on his hands and knees, like a skittish dog. "Get away from me."

Anger kidnaps Cynthia's senses. Standing, she pulls up her jeans. "You were just lying there ready to go, so I got on." Cynthia snickers.

"You're sick."

"Me? How many guys lay sprawled on the floor passed out naked with a woody?"

"Get out of here." Toth screams.

"I'm not going anywhere until you tell me why you screamed that skanks name."

"I'll tell you why. Because it's her I want, not you. She's everything I see in a woman and more."

"Good luck. She doesn't even give you the time of day."

"That's what you think." Toth scrambles to his feet, and grabbing the table cloth, wraps it around himself. "She was just here."

"You're lying."

"No, I'm not. That's her beer over there." Hector points.

"See?"

"That doesn't prove anything, you jerk. It doesn't even look like it's been touched."

Seething hatred swells in Cynthia. How dare he cheat on her like this, she, Cynthia Scotchland, the mother of his future children. None of that matters now. All she cares about is teaching Toth a lesson, one he'll never forget.

"Maybe you're right, Hector. I should just accept the fact that you've gone your own way, and that we're not a couple anymore."

Toth rubs the back of his head, feeling a lump rise to the surface. "Good, I'm glad you're coming to your senses. Now, if you'll leave, I'll forget about you abusing me while I was passed out."

"I couldn't resist." Cynthia's voice seems far away. Wrapping herself in her coat, she slithers to the door. "See you Hector, it's been real." Glancing down at the floor, she laughs. "You know Toth, if you're going to eat cereal, you shouldn't be such a pig about it. Look, there are Fruit Loops everywhere."

Cynthia sweeps out into the night, and Toth wonders what the psycho has up her sleeve, telling himself to remember to check his tires later.

Scampering to the bathroom, Hector pulls aside the shower curtain, and steps into the tub. Sniffing, he can smell her scent embedded in his skin. Scrubbing his hard body under the spraying jets, Hector tries to wash the stink off. How dare she molest him like that when he can't even enjoy it.

Smiling as he rinses, Toth stops for a moment, thinking

he hears something. He swears that if Cynthia has come back, he'll kill her and bury her in the backyard.

Rushing out of the soothing shower, Toth reaches for a towel and twists it around his midsection. Stumbling into the dark living room, he doesn't see anything unusual swaying in the shadows.

Turning back to the still running taps, Hector suddenly feels something pierce the nape of his neck, as his knees collapsed beneath him. His eyes open in horror as he utters his last words. "But why?"

Staggering up to his apartment, Jimmy Prescott reaches the landing and wipes his face with a snowy scarf. "How'd I get so drunk?" he asks, hugging the brown bag against his chest.

Digging deep into his coat pocket, he fishes out the keys. Bobbling the ring between his freezing fingers, he almost drops them into the drift below.

Unlocking the door, Jimmy shivers as the darkness kisses him. Fumbling for the light switch, he flicks it on, blackness follows the echoing click. Nervously trying a few more times, Jimmy realizes the power is out.

"Damn-it," he swears, scrambling across the floor to the buffet. In his hurry, Jimmy cracks his shin against a chair, and almost falling, safe guards the booze.

Yanking a drawer open, his pumping adrenaline almost makes him pull it all the way out, but he catches it before the contents spill to the floor. Shuffling a few items aside, he finally finds a tapered candle, figuring it will have to do.

Now for a holder.

Spotting an empty beer bottle on the end table, Jimmy picks it up and sniffs. A slight scent, but it'll do. Cramming the candle into the decanters mouth, he flicks his Bic, and watches as a small spark appears. Sensing the lighter is almost spent, Jimmy holds his breath as he lights the wick, watching it flutter into a flame.

The empty walls are filled with an antique white color, soft, and grandmotherly. Jimmy stumbles over to the couch and rips a beer from the plastic harness. Twisting the cap off the Jack Daniel's, he takes a shot, washing it down with the Bud.

Going over to the window, he opens the port and stashes the bag on the stoop. Easing the pane back down, making sure to leave a little crack so it can't freeze shut. Jimmy shivers, and sashays to the fireplace to build a fire.

The blaze is going in no time, as Jimmy stands in front of the warmth, thinking to himself how good life really is, even if he is alone.

❋   ❋   ❋

Circling the room, Sheriff Anderson rips the yellow tape from the roll and ties the end to a chair. He hears Mira weeping in the distance. The whole scenario is a little off beat, Jon thinks, wondering who'd want to kill Billy Mendelson.

Standing still in the middle of the living room, Jon turns clockwise, a quarter at a time. By now he has gotten used to the stench, and the air seems sweetened with the aroma.

He's amazed at his calmness.

The murderer must have known Billy, he concludes, due to no signs of a struggle, and the only thing that's unusual are the Fruit Loops sprinkled everywhere. Maybe it's some sort of busted drug deal, Jon contemplates, lumbering to the kitchen to ask Mira a few questions.

Poking his head around the corner, Jon sees the three of them sitting at the table, their hands wrapped around steaming cups of coffee. Mira notices him first.

Standing, she says, "Jon, come, sit down, let me pour you a cup of coffee." Mira's always been an attentive hostess.

"No, no, Mira, you stay," nudging Mark. "My deputy will be more than happy to get me some." Jon slugs his arm. "Right, Mark?"

"Yeah, oh sure, right, Jon." Rubbing his bicep, and whimpering. "You don't have to bruise me." The young man stands up, and Jon sits down in his warm chair.

"Mark, then I want you to take Delores upstairs, and put her in Mira's room. After that, you go watch the body. I need to ask Mrs. Mendelson some questions."

"Why can't I stay with Delores? Billy's not going anywhere."

Delores snorts, and then covers her mouth in embarrassment. "I'm sorry, Mira."

"*Now*, Mark." The sheriff's voice is firm and direct, and

setting the cup down in front of his boss, Mark Pickens grabs his wife's hand and leads her out of the room.

Turning around, Deputy Pickens replies. "You know how I feel about dead bodies after finding that one as a child. Remember?"

"Yes, I do, Mark." Jon's tone a little softer. "But this is your job, and you have to obey my orders."

"Ah, come on."

"Mark, you're pushing my last nerve. Just go do what I say." He whispers harshly under his breath, annoyed that the women have to see his deputy defy him.

Deputy Pickens stares down at his feet and shuffles them, like a little boy just reprimanded. Feeling guilty, Jon strolls over to him and places his hand on his deputies shoulder. "Listen Mark, this is important. I covered the body, so you won't see it. All I'm asking, is that you go in there, sit down, and keep guard."

"I don't know why I can't ask Mrs. Mendelson the questions."

Jon's about to blow a gasket. He can't believe Mark is acting like such an adolescent.

Grabbing his arm, he leads him out of the kitchen.

"Ouch, Jon, you're hurting me."

"Shut up!" He pushes him against the wall, pointing his finger at the shaking man. "You listen to me, and you listen to me good. I don't have time for these games. Either you do what I say, or you can leave and start looking for another job. My gosh, you're acting like a coward in front of your wife. What kind of man are you?"

"A scared one, Jon. I don't mean nothing by it, it's just memories." Mark straightens his posture. "I'll go do it, I certainly don't want to lose my job." He pokes his head into the kitchen. "Delores, come on, I want to show you the upstairs."

"Is there a television in the bedroom, I get bored fast." She asks, glancing back at Mira who nods her head yes.

Jon returns to the kitchen and sits down at the table across from Mira. Reaching for her hands laying there, he covers them with his massive paws. "Mira, I'm sorry about that. I don't know what gets into him. I guess this being the first real crime we've worked on, he's a little nervous."

"That's okay, Jon, I understand. I'm sure you must be a little bit at nerves end, too."

"Well, to be honest, yes." He takes a sip of coffee. "Now Mira, I need to ask you some standard questions, it won't take long, so if you can just bear with me."

"Anything to help find my son's murderer."

"Okay, then. Now, Mira, when did you last see Billy?"

"Earlier this morning, I made him breakfast, and then I had to leave. He was sitting right here eating his eggs and bacon."

"Did you say he was eating bacon and eggs?"

"Yes, that's his usual meal in the morning."

"Did he ever eat cereal?"

"Seldom."

"And if he did, what kind would he have?"

"Always cornflakes. Billy's kind of set in his food patterns." She chokes a tear back.

"So, you never saw him eating Fruit Loops."

"Oh, heavens no. That cereal is awful."

Jon touches the ringlets in his pocket. "Was he expecting anyone to come over today?"

"I think Candy Jane was stopping by. But she's here all the time." Mira stops for a moment. "Billy did seem a little agitated about something, though. I think he and Candy are/were having a little spat."

"Did they fight often?"

"Oh, I wouldn't call it fighting. It was more like Candy trying to light a fire under Billy, you know, trying to motivate him to start making something of his life." Tears begin to fall again from the grieving mother. "I certainly didn't do a very good job raising my son, did I?"

"You did a great job, Mira. Billy had a mind of his own, and he just didn't want to use it." Jotting something down in his notebook, he studies Mira for a moment. "Now, you say you think they were arguing?"

"Yes, I believe Billy was going to ask Candy Jane to marry him, and there was a little tension between them because of it."

"So, Candy Jane wasn't in favor of the idea?"

"I guess not, at least it didn't seem like it to Billy. But he was going to try anyway." Mira wipes her eyes. "She would never do anything like this, Jon. Candy Jane's one of the sweetest girls I know. Just because she's smart enough to recognize that my son and her didn't have a future, doesn't make her a murderer."

"Do you know the last time they saw each other?"

"I think last night, because when I got home I heard voices coming from Billy's room, so I just naturally assumed it was her."

"She didn't spend the night? Instead, drove home in a blizzard, that doesn't make sense to me."

"Well, Sheriff, if you saw my sons room, you'd know why."

Jon continues. "Do you know if she came back today."

"No, she wasn't here when I left."

"And did Billy ever have any other friends stop by for a visit?"

"Not that I know of. He really didn't have a whole lot of acquaintances. Plus, I have no idea what he does when I'm not here."

"Now, when you say you heard voices coming from Billy's room last night, what kind of tones were they?"

"A little yelling, mostly on Billy's part, but nothing came of it. They quieted down right away."

I bet they did, Jon thinks out of the blue, feeling an unusual twinge of jealousy.

"Mira, do you know if he had any enemies?"

Mira contemplates for a moment. "I really can't say, Jon. I know he started acting like a real jerk after he inherited all that money from his father. But I don't believe he offended anyone to the point where you could call them a foe."

Sheriff Jon Anderson is baffled. "Excuse me, Mira." Standing, Jon returns to the living room and relieves his deputy, telling him to retrieve his wife, and then meet him back in the kitchen.

Studying the form lumped on the couch, he eases over, and removes the blanket from the corpse. Reaching for the camera, Jon shoots several photos before snagging a pair of rubber gloves out of his pocket, and snapping them on, carefully lifts Billy's head, searching for the entry wound. He sees the blood crusted hole immediately, and realizes Billy never knew what hit him. "Poor guy," Jon whispers and gently sets his head back down.

The killer has to know exactly where to place the weapon so that it will pierce him directly at the cervical, puncturing his brain upon entry. This isn't a random murder, this is premeditated, and Jon knows those are the ones who usually get away.

"Sheriff."

Mark Pickens voice startles Jon out of his thoughts, he slightly jumps. "Yes, Mark."

"Sheriff, Gear's on the walkie-talkie and he says he can't get through to the State Police. I guess the radio's down."

Jon recalls the last city council meeting and how they had voted against purchasing a newer model, saying the extra expense isn't necessary, and that he can make do.

"Irony at its best, Mark."

"Huh?" Mark burps out.

"Oh, nothing." Surveying the room, Jon turns back to Mark." Well, we can't leave the body here all night. We're going to have to take it out back and put it in the garage."

"You mean, we have to touch it?"

"Yes, Mark, it's no big deal."

"I don't know why we just can't leave it."

"Because, Mark, we have to keep it in a cold place."

"Just turn down the heat."

Shaking his head, Jon feels a ripple of pain crease his brow. "Mark, just do as I say."

"Jon? What's going on?"

Turning, he sees Mira standing in the doorway. "All the phone lines are down, we can't get a signal on the cells, and the radio at the station is on the fritz, so we're unable to get through to the State Police. I thought it best if we move the body into the garage, if that's all right with you."

"No, that's fine, you do what you have to do, but you might want to put him in the shed. There's more room." Mira quiets for a moment. "If you want I can go out there and fix a place."

"That won't be necessary. We can take care of it." Side-eyeing Mark. "Deputy Pickens, do you mind checking out the shed?"

"Yes, sir." He sarcastically salutes as he waves for Dolores to follow him.

"Let's go, honey."

This time, Jon decides to let them be, he's getting tired and wants to go home so he can think about this quietly. "Hey, Mira, why don't you come spend the night with me and Carol. There's plenty of room."

She puts her hand on his arm. "No, Jon, if it's all right with you, I'd rather just stay here, you know, close to Billy. It's our last night together."

"I suppose it's all right. I mean it's your house and all. Just promise me you'll stay away from the crime scene. I'll be back in the morning, okay?"

Mira Mendelson stands on her tip-toes and kisses him on the cheek. "Thanks, Jon." She retreats toward the staircase. "I'm just going to go to bed, now, I'm exhausted, and I can't do this anymore."

"That's fine, Mira, I'll lock up before I leave."

"Thanks again, Jon."

She disappears into the dark shadows of the stairwell, and for a brief instant, Jon wonders if Mira Mendelson has killed her own son. She could have planted the weapon before leaving, knowing exactly where he'd lay down after breakfast. Stage it as an outside murder. Jon shakes the thought out of his head; it's too uncharacteristic for Mira, he grew up with her, and knows better.

Gazing out the window while waiting for Mark, Sheriff Anderson sees the outline of the Swanson's house about a half mile away. Snow rips at it, and Jon watches as swirls of smoke rise from the chimney. The place is pitch dark, and he feels shivers race down his body, as he turns around quickly.

"Hey, Mira," he yells up the stairs."

She stops and looks down at him. "Yes?"

"Do you have a generator?"

"Yes, as soon as the power goes out, it kicks on. I tell you that machine has paid for itself time and again."

"I bet. Night, Mira."

"Good-night, Jon."

Sheriff Anderson listens to her light footsteps taper down the hall. A door shuts softly, as a sudden still silence unsettles him.

"Okay, Jon, it's ready."

For the second time tonight Jon Anderson is startled out of his thoughts, his heart clumps against his chest.

"What'd I tell you about sneaking up on people, Mark?"

"I can't help it if I walk softly and carry a big stick."

Delores giggles, and entwines her arm within her husbands, gazing at him admirably. "Sweety, you're so funny." She kisses him lovingly on the cheek.

Feeling a little nauseous from Delores' display of affection, Jon intervenes. "Okay, Billy Jack, tell the Missus to go sit in the kitchen while we finish up here. Then the two of you can go home."

"Oh, goody, Mark." She peck kisses him again. "This place is giving me the creeps."

"Okay, honey, just go to the kitchen, so we can take care of this, all right?"

Delores scampers away. "Hurry up."

Jon shakes his head, and says, "Come on, let's get this over with."

The two men hoist the body off the couch, and notice a grayish stain on the beige cover. The smell is unbearable as Mark spits. "My gosh, Jon, I really don't know if I can do this."

"Just hold your breath until we get outside, okay. Whatever you do, don't drop him."

Hurrying out the door, Jon and Mark slip and slide to the shed, and laying Billy's body on the tarp covered floor, Sheriff Anderson retrieves a blanket from a shelf and covers the corpse.

"Come on, Mark, let's get out of here," Jon says, as they both stand in silence gazing at the mound.

Closing and paddle-locking the door behind them, Jon wraps his arm around his deputy's shoulder. "Hey, Mark, I'm sorry if you think I was a little rough on you, I just didn't want to mess anything up."

"No, I understand, Jon. I guess I was kind of being a dumb-ass."

"Okay, then. Why don't you gather Delores and head home. I don't think I'll need you anymore tonight."

"Are you sure, Sheriff?"

"Yeah, go ahead."

Deputy Pickens runs for the house. "Delores, hey Delores, get your things, we can go."

He's acting like a school boy let out of detention early, Jon thinks, smiling. Lumbering into the house, he returns to the crime scene. More cereal lines the couch, and Jon laughs to himself, realizing the only clue he has to Mongoose Falls first homicide is a handful of Fruit Loops.

The jail house is pitch dark as Deputy Gear Larson moves his hand along the wall trying to find the light switch. Flipping it up, the room dances with shadows. "Oh, hell," he hisses, figuring the whole town must be in a blackout.

Gangling over to the cabinet, he opens the swinging doors, and grabbing two Coleman lanterns, sets them on the desk. Fumbling in his pocket, he pulls out a crumpled book of matches. Striking one against the sandpaper strip, he lights the lamps, and watches as the room suddenly illuminates into a soft yellow glow.

Picking up the phone, Gear isn't surprised to hear silence. At least he can say he checked in case the sheriff asks. "It's all a part of the job." He hears Jon's favorite point loud and clear.

Wind wrestled trees bang against the windows making Gear jump. Another blow like that and the branch will shatter the glass, he frets, eyeing the ham radio in the corner. Picking up the mike, he turns the switch on and squawks into the mouth piece. "Hello, anyone out there?" Dead air envelopes him, like a San Francisco fog. "Hello!"

Now he'll have to call Jon on the walkie-talkie. Unholstering the hand device, he holds it to his mouth. "Sheriff, come in, do you read me? This is Gear at the station." There's a crackling sound before he hears Mark Pickens' voice come over the waves.

"Gear, hey it's Mark, what's happening."

"Is the sheriff around?" Gear's voice is tight. The two deputies had a falling out a few months ago, right before Mark got married. The *groom-to-be*, accused his *used-to-be-best -friend,* of making a move on Delores, which he never did. It was incidental contact.

"No, he's with Mrs. Mendelson. Can I give him a message?"

"Yes, tell him the phones are out and the radio is on the blink again, so I can't get through to the State Police."

"Okay, I'll tell him." Mark pauses for a moment and then lies. "Hey, Jon wants you to stay at the office until you hear from him. He told me to tell you that when you checked in."

"What for, there's nothing to do here?"

"I don't know. Why don't you ask him when he contacts you. Ten-four buddy, over and out."

"Over and out." Gear, disgruntled, sits down in Jon's chair behind his desk. Plopping his feet on top of the pile of paper work, Gear wonders, now what's he going to do?

There's no electricity, so he can't watch TV or listen to the radio. Maybe that's a good thing, Gear figures, he can use a little peace and quiet. Plus, this is a lot better than being at home with his nagging girlfriend. Lately, it seems like she hates everything, and Gear's beginning to believe that there's nothing he can do to make her happy.

He's been thinking about breaking it off with her, but is a little afraid to. Gear knows she's a hair-trigger, and one wrong move and he's toast. Her temper is one to avoid at all costs. The good thing is, she's a tiger in bed, and if there's one reason to hang onto a broad, it's that.

Caught in his daydream, he doesn't hear the back door open, or see the silhouetted figure slide across the dim wall. A nibbling chill rakes across his hairy neck. The intruder sneaks up behind him, and flips his chair back, sending the six foot man tumbling to the floor. He quickly takes a four point stance, his high school football instincts taking charge, and glares into the darkness.

"Who's there?" His voice cracks. Squinting toward a

creaking floor board, Gear grabs the flashlight and shines it in the direction. "What are you doing here?"

The visitor saunters over to him, and rubs her body against his. "Oh, honey pie, I couldn't stand to be away from you any longer. I'm so horny, I need you to take care of me." She begins licking his neck, and fingering his groin.

He slaps her hand away. "Stop that, the sheriff's going to be back any time and he won't like it if he finds you here, so you'd better leave."

"Well, he can join in too. Wouldn't it turn you on to see me with another man?" Her roaming hands and rushing fingers fumbling with his zipper.

She has a point, Gear thinks, but not with Sheriff Anderson. He slaps her again, this time, not so hard. "Not now, babe, save it for later."

"I don't know if I can wait, I feel a little out of control, Gear." She begins gyrating on his thigh.

Pushing her away, she stumbles into the file cabinet. "What's your problem? I told you *not now*. Jon will be back any minute. You gotta go."

"I don't think he'll be back from the Mend---," she stops short and starts to walk away.

Gear reaches for her arm. "What were you going to say?" Gear squeezes a little tighter. "How do you know he's at the Mendelson's?"

She forcefully rips out of his grasp. "For God's sake, Gear." Her voice, solid and raised. "I saw his sled parked in front of the house. What's the big deal?" She turns away from him. "Listen, I think you're right, I'd better split."

"Why don't you go wait for me at my apartment, I should be there within the hour."

Gear's voice softens. "And hey, I'm sorry, things are just a little weird around here, ya know?" He draws up next to her, and pulls her close. Lowering his head, he kisses her gently. "Just be careful out there, okay."

"Yeah, I guess."

Deputy Larson watches as his girlfriend of six months vanishes into the white-out. Maybe he should have let her stay, it's getting rather dangerous, but then she did make it here on her own. It's a good thing he sent her away, she was starting to get to him, a minute more and who knows what might have happened.

Sitting back in the sheriff's chair, Gear wonders why Cynthia would be driving by the Mendelson's, she lives on the other side of town.

"Whatever!" Gear whispers to himself, and closing his eyes, listens to the thrashing ice pellets nick at the windows.

❋   ❋   ❋

Candice Jane Cane is running scared. The roads are slick and icy. She can feel her bare threaded tires slide back and forth as she crawls down the deserted streets.

It's taking her longer to get to Jimmy's than she anticipated. Her mind is getting fuzzy, a little dizzy from the constant brightness of the snow. She leans closer to the window, an opaque mist closes in, dimming the headlights.

"Can this day get anymore unbelievable?" She whisper,

shaking her head as she recaps the events. Did she really kill Toth? She keeps rewinding the whole scene, frame after frame, and it all seems surreal. Candy knows she's not at fault, here. He was attacking her. Still, she killed a man.

Stopping in front of Jimmy's house, Candy Jane turns off the car, and pats the dash-board. Counting to three, and then getting out, she burrows through the foot of snow, and just as she reaches the stairs, hears meowing.

Wheeling to her right, Candy sees a shivering kitty beneath a snow capped bush. Noticing the feline's whiskers are turning to ice, she scoops her up out of the thick white powder, and holds the freezing kitten to her chest. She begins purring immediately, and nuzzles her face into Candy's coat.

"Poor, baby! Don't you worry, everything's all right now, Candy's here." She feels her heart swell with warmth.

Climbing the stairs to Jimmy's apartment, she raps on the door and listens as he shuffles through the vestibule and answers. His eyes are glazed, and she knows he's been drinking.

For a minute, Jimmy doesn't recognize Candy; she sees bewilderment etched on his face. Then, familiarity slaps him, and he slurs. "Candy Jane, what are you doing here? Are you crazy driving in this weather?" He glances down at her full arms. "And why did you bring a date?" Jimmy begins laughing; Candy sees no humor.

She slithers past him. "You're not funny."

"My, my, a hearty welcome to you to." Jimmy pushes the door shut, and watches as Candy Jane struts over to the fireplace, setting the kitten down in front of the blaze.

"Do you know who's cat this is? I found her in the bushes nearly frozen to death."

Jimmy moves closer, and scrunches down. "I don't know, I've never seen it before." He strokes the wet fur, and then flicks hair off his fingers.

"She must've been out there for a while." Reaching up, Candy grabs the towel Jimmy hands to her. She swathes the feline with the soft terry cloth, listening to purrs of delight. "Yeah, pretty kitty, everything will be all right now. Candy's here."

"You're taking it with you when you leave, right?" Jimmy picks up a can of beer and downs it. "And by the way, *what,* are you doing here?"

Leaning back against the wall, Candy studies Jimmy Prescott. His eyes are half mast, and she can tell he's already three sheets to the wind. What good will it do her to confide in him when he won't even recall it tomorrow. And he certainly is not going to be of any help tonight.

"I'm on my way home from Sven's and I thought I'd stop and apologize for earlier."

"Apology accepted. What were you doing at Sven's?"

"I went into work."

"Didn't they call you?"

"I wasn't home, I was at Billy's." A lump formed in her throat.

"And how is the twisted bastard?" Jimmy tries to take another sip off his beer, and realizing its empty, stands and asks. "Hey, do you want a Bud. I only have a couple, but you can have one."

The thought of a beer makes her nauseous. "No thanks, Jimmy." Candy replies, feeling a little spiteful toward Jimmy after his comment. "I have to drive, and the roads are getting really bad."

"Are the plows out yet?"

"I've seen a couple, but it's hard for them to keep up. This is a doozy of a storm." Sliding up the wall, she continues. "As a matter of fact, I should get going." She glances down at the sleeping cat. "Hey, do you mind keeping the kitty till the morning, I don't want to traumatize her anymore than she already has been. Then we can find out who she belongs to."

Jimmy bends down and pets the wrapped cat, reminding him of a drowned rat. "Yeah, sure, I'm not going to put her back outside in the cold. Plus, we can keep each other company."

Patting Jimmy on the back as she leaves, Candy Jane says. "Great, but don't get too friendly, I know how you are when you drink." She snickers.

"You know me better than that. She's a *she*, remember. I'm an exclusive male only bride." Jimmy searches his friends face for a moment. "Are you sure you're okay, honey?"

"Yeah, I'm just a little tired that's all."

"Well, you go home and get some sleep, okay."

"I will." Candy's glad Jimmy didn't re-open the subject about Billy. "I'll call you tomorrow. night!"

"Wait just a minute, young lady. You're not leaving

without a hug."

Hesitantly, Candy goes over to him. "Just a little one, and no breast pressing."

"You're no fun." He kisses her on both cheeks, barely hugging her. "There, how's that?"

She steps back before he decides to really hug her, and looks up at the clock. It's almost seven. "I really have to get going."

"Be careful out there."

"I will. Have fun with the cat."

"She'll probably sleep all night. I know I will."

Remaining on the stoop for a moment after Jimmy closes the door, Candy Jane wonders why she's being so aloof about things. Is she in shock? Have the circumstances not really set in yet, and when they do, will she have a total breakdown. After all, she did just kill a man and yet, she's more concerned about the well being of a cat.

A hollowness echoes in her heart as she pulls away from Jimmy's house.

Deputy Larson snarls as he straddles the snow mobile. Nothing's going right tonight. First, he had to deal with his crazy girlfriend, and now he has to go stand guard at the Mendelson house in case the murderer comes back. Gear's curious why Pickens just didn't stay.

The whole thing is ridicules. Someone being murdered in Mongoose Falls. Things like that just don't happen here,

Gear frets, as he starts the ski-doo and tightens his scarf for the frigid ride.

Billy Mendelson is kind of a klutz, and probably fell on something, or took too many pills, and killed himself accidentally. That's all it is. He races across the snow filled fields enjoying the solitude, and telling himself that Sheriff Anderson owes him big.

Sheriff Jon Anderson is shivering so badly that he thinks he'll chip a tooth if they chatter against each other any harder. He's never been so cold, and knows he needs to find shelter to warm up in, and fast.

He's still a little unsure about his decision to have Gear keep guard at Mira's, but Jon feels a little safer having someone there. Who knows, maybe it's a botched robbery, and the culprit plans on going back tonight.

Better safe than sorry, is his mantra.

Trying not to think about how numb his body is, Jon races across the virgin snow. The clouds are breaking apart, casting bright stars glittering in the black sky. He spots Hector Toth's house up the way and decides to stop there to unthaw. Slowing down in front of the trailer, Jon is sure Hector won't mind. Who'd say *no* to the law?

Maneuvering the sled around to the back of the dark house, he hopes someone is home as he hoofs it to the porch. Noticing the door is swinging open, Jon places his hand on his gun as an eerie sensation ripples through him.

Quiet buzzes all around him as he steps onto the landing. The absence of noise makes Jon recall Simon and Garfunkle's *Sound of Silence*.

"Toth, you in here?"

Sliding the flashlight off his belt, Sheriff Anderson shines the beam around the kitchen. It's filthy, which doesn't surprise Jon. He proceeds to the dining room, his steps crunching the garbage on the floor. He lowers the light to see what he's walking on, and sees a line of Fruit Loops. Following the trail, he discovers Hector Toth laying motionless in the middle of the room.

"Oh, geeze." Jon pants, shaking his head and slowly moving toward the body. He already knows Toth is dead, there's no doubting lifelessness.

Snapping his second pair of gloves out of his pocket, Jon rolls Hector over and inspects the nape of his neck. There, too, is a small puncture mark, just like Billy's, the blood already starting to dry.

Resting his head back, Jon's still for a moment. "Can there be a serial killer loose?" An internal voice asks him. Raking his hand through his hair, Jon shakes his head back and forth. He needs to get help. Someone other than his two deputy dogs.

Studying Hector's torso, he notices that the dead man has a towel wrapped around his midsection, and his hair is damp. He must've been taking a shower when something made him get out. Suddenly, Jon hears water running and goes into the bathroom. He watches as a jet stream sprays out of the nozzle. Placing his hand under the water, and feeling it's coldness, Jon concludes that the shower must've been running for awhile.

Returning to the body, he bends over and touches the skin. It's clammy warm, the kind mosquitoes are attracted to. Wiping his hand on his pants, he figures the murder must have taken place within the hour.

Resting his palm on his revolver, Jon is suspicious that the killer might still be here.

Casing the rest of the house, he finds no one, nor nothing, except for more ringlets. Joking with himself, he says out loud. "Great, I have Fruit Loops the Serial Killer on my hands." He begins laughing hysterically, thick tears fall from his eyes, as the tension at last starts to invade him.

Searching for another baggie in his pocket, he writes, *Hector Toth*, and carefully places several of the sugar bits inside. Studying the pink, blue, orange, green cereal, he can't think of anything, or one, that the two men have in common that would make them both targets.

He'll have to find the connection, but right now all he wants to do is get home, and lay down in bed. There, he can think more clearly. Covering Toth's body with a blanket, Jon heads toward the door. He knows he has to figure these cases out fast, because by the looks of it, this guy is on a murdering rampage, and Sheriff Anderson fears for the unknown third.

❄ ❄ ❄

Candy Jane Cane shuffles along the slick sidewalk, trying

to maintain her balance. Holding onto the black iced rail, leading to the porch of Town Hall, Candy lunges to the top. "This is ridicules," she spits. Why are these things happening to her? Why can't Jimmy be sober for once?

Well, at least there's a light on here, maybe she can at last get some help.

Twisting the ridged handle, Candy's annoyed when it won't turn. Trying it with her other hand, the brass knob clicks, and as the door opens, she steps into the dimly lit room.

"Hello, anyone around?" Her words bounce off the empty walls.

Skipping down the two steps and over to the wood stove, she perches in front of the small fire. The room reminds her of the Mayberry RFD jailhouse. Giggling to herself, Candy suddenly feels a little tipsy, even though she's had nothing to drink.

It must be the stress, trying to comfort herself.

Warming, she feels her veins begin to defrost, and her fingers tingle. A sensation she's always disliked. Grabbing the lit lantern off the desk, Candy heads to the bathroom to run her fingers under some cold water. The remedy usually helps.

Turning on the faucets, Candy's breath is stolen as she hears the front door open. Hopefully it's someone who can assist her. Reaching for the door handle, Candy stops short as the lantern flutters out, and the bathroom fills with darkness.

❋　❋　❋

Deputy Larson maneuvers the snowmobile around to the side, noticing there's a car parked in front. "Who in the hell would be out in this kind of weather?" He questions, becoming slightly peeved that someone is here.

He's made the decision to come back to the office, and then just make occasional trips to the Mendelson's to check things out. He doesn't see the sense of staying there. Plus, it gives him the creeps being in a house where a death has occurred.

He stomps into the shadowy office, as the old snow packed roof creaks under the weight. Scratching his head, Gear thought he left a lantern burning, but guessed he must've blown it out instinctively. Searching for a flashlight, he locates one on the cabinet.

"*We all live in a yellow submarine, yellow submarine*," Gear mouths the words to the Beatles tune, one of his favorites. Switching on the torch and expecting a beam to appear, Gear slaps the device against his palm, trying to shake some light free. Unable to, he realizes the batteries must be drained. In his frustration, he doesn't hear the back door open, or the rubber sucking soles against the concrete floor approach him.

He doesn't feel the stealth weapon pierce the softness at the back of his neck, and then puncture his brain. Gear Larson's last thoughts are, how sad it is there won't ever be a Beatles reunion.

❄ ❄ ❄

Candy Jane can't believe the flame flickered out. She's so afraid of the dark, she can already sense fear begin rippling through her veins. Hearing Deputy Larson humming, she's overcome with instant relief. Slowly opening the door, she freezes, watching as a figure tip-toes up behind him, puncturing the back of his neck with what looks like a long, thick needle.

Gasping, Candy ducks down, feeling her hairs stand on end, as Deputy Larson slumps to the floor. Meeting his dead eyes for an instant, she crawls into the hidden corner. She thinks she hears footsteps running away, far away, somewhere in a distant place. Candy's head begins to spin, and she suddenly passes out.

Coming too, Candy is dazed, and at first doesn't know where she is. A deep stillness fills the room, as she listens to the crackling fire coming from the stove. Slithering over to the wall, she's unsure of how long she's been unconscious.

Peering through the small sliver in the open door, Candy sees Deputy Larson's dead body, his eyes still shocked open. This time the stare has little affect on her. Holding her breath for a moment, she listens for any sounds, and hearing none, decides to get the hell out of there.

What are the chances she'd be involved with three deaths in one night? Shaking her head, Candy feels numb. She can't believe this turn of fortune. These events are wild, situations she never thought of encountering. It's as though the Karma Queen decided to give her a big dose of *what goes around comes around*. But Candy can't think of anything she's done so bad, that warrants this wrath.

Crawling out of the bathroom, and scanning the office, she bolts for the door. Why is she so scared? She didn't do anything. Maybe she should just wait until the sheriff comes back, and explain everything. He'll have to believe her; she's never been in any trouble before. Plus, she's always felt kind of a connection with him.

Something nags at her though, pin-pointing the terror nerve, and not paying attention, Candy slips on the frozen steps, tumbling down the small flight of stairs. Luckily, the mounds of snow pad her fall. Groaning with exhaustion, she hoists herself up.

Reaching her car without any more incidents, Candy lays her head on the chilling steering wheel and tries to decide what to do. Maybe the best thing, she believes, is to return to Jimmy's. Hopefully he's sobered up a little, and can be of some help now.

Ramming the tired car into gear, she fishtails down the treacherous street. "Nobody told me there'd be days like this." Candy whispers. "Oh, Mr. Lennon, if you only knew."

5

Sheriff Jon Anderson is wound tighter than a spinning top, as he speeds to the jail house. Hoping he can get the radio working, Jon knows this case is about to blow wide open and he needs help, and now. Slowing for a curve, Jon tries to think of ideas, maybe find a hummer, or a county snow plow, and drive down to Minnetonka where a station is centered. But that's insane, he can barely see fifteen feet in front of him. And without phones or radios, his predicament is quickly worsening.

Reaching the front of the building, Jon notices that the door is wide open, and curses Gear under his breath for not locking it before he left for the Mendelson's. The moment he steps into the dim office, though, he senses something is wrong. Seeing Gear's bright red coat tossed over his desk chair, Jon wonders where his deputy is.

Moving forward, he jams his frozen toes on the edge of

the desk. Yelping, Jon hops around on one leg, not paying attention to where he's going. Backing up, he falls over Gear's dead body. Cracking his skull on the concrete floor, Jon sees bright sparkles fluttering in front of his eyes. Shaking his head, he examines his scalp for a lump, and finds one already forming.

Angry, Jon shoves Gear with his foot. "Get up, you idiot." His boot thumps against the hardening torso. Jon sits up, and touches Deputy Larson's leg. "Gear?" Even before he speaks, Jon knows he'll not get a reply.

Rising, he hears something crunch beneath his knee, and glancing down, scoops up the multi-color cereal. "Fruit Loops!" The severity of the situation slaps Sheriff Anderson across the face. Jon lays his ear on Gear's ribs and listens for a heartbeat, his chest echoes hallow. "Fruit Loops the Serial Killer, has struck again."

Jon feels like he's drowning, he can't breathe. His chest is heavy and his eyes blur over with tears. His brain seems like it's short circuiting. He's having a panic attack, and he needs to calm down. Breathing deeply, and concentrating on his slow breaths, Jon sits back and tries to relax, counting to ten in a whisper.

Tugging his flashlight out of his belt, Sheriff Anderson shines it at the back of Gear's neck. Seeing a nick, he inches over to the body, to observe more closely. He sees it's a small puncture mark, exactly like Billy and Toth's.

What's going on here?

There is absolutely no connection between Gear and the other two. No similarities what-so-ever. Gear was a popular, well liked man around town. Why would anyone want to do this to him? A teardrop rolls down Sheriff Anderson's face and he swipes it away.

Stabling himself, Jon stands up, canvassing the room. These murders are getting a little too close to home, and if anything, Jon Anderson is a man of determination.

A flicker catches his eye, and bending over, he picks up the sparkling object with a handkerchief. Holding it in the air, Jon realizes it must be the murder weapon. Gear's blood still stains the blade. The killer must've dropped it.

Feeling his heart leap as he studies the miniature stiletto, he figures the instrument must've been hand designed. He's never seen anything like this before, noticing the precision of the blade.

What a stroke of luck, Jon thinks, laying the clue on his desk, as he snaps a pair of rubber gloves on. There might be more evidence laying around, and he doesn't want to contaminate it.

His search brings him nothing, and soon Jon begins to feel the fatigue of the day swallow him. Sitting down in his chair, he closes his eyes for a moment, promising himself to just rest them for a minute, and then he'll get back to work. His mind twists into nonsense. Cartoon clowns race through his carnival thoughts, kidnapping his consciousness.

Dreams swim through him and then drain like noodles in a colander. At some point he hears himself trying to tell his mind to wake up, that this is not the time to be napping, but his brain doesn't listen. Resting his head back, Sheriff Jon Anderson falls deep and hard into sleep.

❋   ❋   ❋

Candy Jane lumbers into Jimmy's apartment, tired and scared. She wasn't able to see who the guy was, but remembers his stature, tall and gangly, almost like a growing teenage boy. Candy tries to think of anybody she knows who fits that description, but draws a blank.

The living room is warm, but Candy still shuffles over to the fireplace and stands in front of the blaze. Shivers race across her as she watches Jimmy, passed out on the Lazy-Boy, the stray cat nestled at his feet.

Exhausted, she enters Jimmy's messy bedroom, and sits down on the made bed. Candy recalls Jimmy once telling her that he always makes his bed, otherwise the devil will sleep in it.

Laying down, Candy thinks about closing the drapes, but figures what sense will that make, there was no one out there anyway. Gazing through the window, she watches as the snow starts falling again, crisp ice floating down. Closing her eyes, Candy Jane begins to cry. Heavy sobs rattle her. She can't believe she's in the middle of these murders. Even though one of them was self defense, she knows they aren't coincidences.

Weariness catches her like a squid on a hook. Rambling fear bounces off her subconscious as Candy Jane slips into a fitful slumber.

❋   ❋   ❋

Mark Pickens rolls off his wife and tries to catch his breath. "Man, Delores, you sure are on fire tonight."

"So are you, Big Daddy."

He likes it when she calls him that.

Delores snuggles up under her groom's arm, all comfy and cozy. "I don't think it was right the way Jon treated you tonight. He was kind of rude and disrespectful, honey."

"He's just doing his job. Why don't we get some sleep?"

Deputy Pickens continues to have flashbacks of Billy's body as he shuts his eyes. He keeps smelling that stench, and for the first time since becoming a deputy, Mark wonders if he's right for the job.

Patricia Moldine's brain is snapping like misguided fireworks. Her heart flutters and beats out of control as she rushes into her quaint studio, throwing her purse across the room, watching as it slams against the paneled wall. Lipstick, keys, compacts crash to the floor like a plane hitting a straight-edged cliff.

Scampering over to the fallen contents, she shuffles through the debris and finds the tan prescription bottle. Popping the top, she shakes two valium out, and tosses them into her mouth, swallowing the pills without water.

Why did she ever move to this god-forsaken town. She knew when she left France, in a hurry, she might add, that the last place the authorities would look is Mongoose Falls, Minnesota. A false identity, a quick dye job, and a few extra pounds, changed her from a French socialite to a washed out bartender. Plus, telling everybody she's from Switzerland helps.

Patricia, calming down, strolls over to the thermostat and cranks it up. To hell with the gas bill, she's freezing and has never been one for the extreme cold. Again she questions her decision to move to the mid-west.

Hector Toth, was a bright spot in her drab gray life, though. Something to look forward to when she woke in the morning. But now, that is gone, and all because of that bitch Cynthia.

Rage boils in her like a witches potion-pot, green-sea suds bubbling over the cast iron caldron. Cynthia Scotchland will get her due, and anyone who tries to get in the way, will be shown no mercy.

Candy Jane Cane twists and turns as restless dreams roll within her:

I'm somewhere, but not sure where. At first I think it's a beach party, but there is no beach. I then realize I'm standing in front of a beat-up car. I lift my head and notice a green missile on a tractor-trailer heading toward me. I see Billy behind the steering wheel. Somehow the weapon comes loose, and is rambling toward me. I step to the side, and it slams into the junker. Then, all of a sudden, I'm gazing down at the Mississippi River. I see a person swimming in the murky water, and am surprised that someone is daring enough to submerge themselves in the polluted sludge. I have to go to the bathroom, and I find one, but it is very crowded. So, I go in search of another. I wonder why every place is so busy, when I discover I am at a carnival. A tale of the ever changing Mississippi comes to me, about how it has a three way split, and it's always forming new streams. I stare at the river, tempted to jump in, but don't believe I can make it across the green mossy rocks protruding from the muddy banks.

Candy Jane awakes with a start, a cold sweat coating her body. A deep sorrow fills her heart as she recalls seeing Billy in her dream. Rubbing her face with her hands, she sits up. Her body feels heavy, achy and sore. What she needs is a hot shower, then things will seem a lot better.

Yesterday's events are fuzzy, kind of like looking at an impressionist's painting, a still life in a still park. Candy wonders what sparked this intellectual thought, figuring it's a subconscious attempt to divert her from the real problem at hand.

Candy Jane knows no one can place her at the murder scenes, so maybe if she just keeps quiet, and acts normal, she'll not be a suspect. What she needs to do is lay low and not bring any attention to herself.

The thought of going to jail scares the crap out of her.

She has to tell someone, though, it's eating her up inside.

But who?

Hearing a faint meow, Candy watches as the orphaned cat sashays into the bedroom. Jumping up on the mattress, the now fluffy dry feline nuzzles her nose in Candy's side. Petting the soft fur, she thinks about her own cat at home. Candy is all too familiar with the attitude awaiting her return.

Listening for any sounds of Jimmy, Candy tip-toes to the door and peers around the corner. He lays there, still in the same position as when he passed out. For a split second, Candy imagines he too, might be dead, but then seeing his chest rise, exhales her held breath in relief.

Yawning and stretching her arms in the air, Candy strides up to the plate glass window, stunned by the snow piled against it. She'll never get out, and the realization of possibly being holed up with Jimmy all day makes her cringe.

What was she thinking coming over here? She should have just gone home, or was she afraid that would be the first place they'd come looking for her. Flashes of being in the big house rips through her mind, casting shivers on her skin. She'll never last in prison.

Squinting at the clock, Candy can't believe it's only three in the morning. Reaching for the afghan at the end of the bed, she spreads it over her and the kitty, still sleeping fitfully. Folding her legs up to her chin, she tucks the blanket around her, trembling as she settles into the warmth.

She begins to feel better as sleep invades her like the British in India. Opening her eyes as the moon peaks through a cloud and lights up the sky, Candy is mesmerized by the dazzling, enchanting, illuminated trees. She believes that if she looks hard enough, she'll see fairies dancing around.

"Yup, everything will be fine in the morning," she whispers. "I know Sheriff Jon will believe me. I know he will." Candy Jane dozes off, as the fire crackles and spits.

❄ ❄ ❄

I'm at my folks house outside Mongoose Falls, asleep in my childhood bedroom. Mark Pickens comes in screaming that my parents and wife have just been hit by an ambulance, and they are all dead. I get up and am in disbelief. I keep saying, "No, no, I must be dreaming." I run downstairs and am very sad. I yell to myself, "wake up," and I think I do in real life, but then I fall right back to sleep and into the dream. Now I'm in the dining room crying and thinking this can't be happening because Dad is already dead. Then I'm trying to find this party, and finally do. I know a few people. Candy Jane is here, and she's drinking vodka out of the bottle. I think she's kind of cute, but drinks too much. Someone then comes up to me and says they saw me last night and I was drunk. I tell them they must be mistaken, because I went to bed early and didn't go out. They say it was me, and I wonder if I had been sleep walking like I used to as a child. I leave the party, and head down this dark, scary, street to find my car. I come upon a man in front of a building, like a cement factory. He tells me he'll show me the way to downtown Mongoose Falls. I follow him through the factory and jump over a trough. He points west and instructs me to go there. Then suddenly, I'm back in Mongoose Falls at my folks house when I realize I have to return to work. I look around the yard and decide to water, even though it's beginning to rain. I glance at the clock and it reads, three-thirty, an hour before I have to leave. I begin hosing the green grass and newly budding garden, and notice there's a new tree where the pear tree used to be. I look at the garage, and think to myself how much I miss my childhood. While

I'm in the garden, I try not to step on the deep green plants.

Sheriff Anderson tumbles out of his chair, waking as he hits the floor. Whipping around, he tries to get his bearings. Standing, he shakes his mind free of the dream, thinking to himself how old he feels.

Rolling his head back and forth, he hears tiny snaps as he catches a glimpse of his visions. He's sad, and figures it's the circumstances surrounding him. Scanning Gear's dead body on the floor, he decides to move the corpse out back in case someone stops by. It's better to keep him cold, anyway, Jon figures.

The lifeless torso is heavy as he drags Gear across the concrete floor. Opening the door, he's greeted with a frigid blast of early morning air and coughs. Sharp stabs pierce his lungs like he just inhaled some dry ice. Rolling the body over to the wall, he locates a blanket, and covers him up.

Standing silent for a moment trying to catch his breath, Jon notices the quietness of the pre-dawn is comforting to his racked nerves. Mark should be here soon, Jon hopes, returning to the office. Then he will go home, say hi to Carol, shower, and try to find some help.

Sitting back down, Jon picks up the baggy with the weapon enclosed, and inspects the stiletto. The knife is for sure custom made, with a needle like blade. He can see how perfectly the instrument will work when it's pin-pointed to the right place.

An instant kill.

"Diabolical," Jon mumbles. Whom, did these three men know that connected them?

Sheriff Anderson twists around quickly as he hears the front door close. He doesn't recognize the figure due to the dim lighting, but as they walk closer, he sees that it's Cynthia Scotchland.

"Miss. Scotchland, may I help you with something?" In the back of Jon's mind he's thinking, how weird is this.

"I came to get my car."

"It must be pretty important to bring you out in this mess, and so early."

"I have an appointment in Minneapolis." She steps forward.

"By the looks of it, maybe you should re-schedule."

"I can't get in touch with them. Even my cell phone isn't working."

Jon glances at the mound of snow covering the jeep. "That's going to take you forever to dig out, are you sure this is the smartest thing to do?"

"Yes, I'll just get Gear to help me." She turns her head, searching for him, and then starts for the back. "Is he in one of the cell's sleeping?"

"Hold on, Cynthia." Jon levels his arm so she can't pass. "You're not allowed back there, plus, Gear's not here."

"Where is he? I saw him earlier. He drove me home on the ski-doo"

"He's working on some official business, and is unavailable. So maybe you should just leave."

Cynthia bolts toward him, and Jon steps back, raising his arm. "Don't come any closer." Jon's a little nervous, he's witnessed this woman jump a man faster than a flee on a dog.

Cynthia stops short, and Jon actually sees a physical change come over her demeanor.

Glaring at him. "Well, Sheriff Anderson, he's my boy-friend, and I have every right to know where he is."

Really, Jon thinks to himself, Gear was tapping this piece of work. Shaking his head, he warns Cynthia. "Ms. Scotch-land the best thing for you to do right now, is leave, before I throw you in jail."

"Oh, yeah, for what?"

"First and foremost, defying the law."

"Right, give me a break. You're not the law. You're just some two-bit sheriff who's never had the ambition to do anything with his life. And the only reason why you're in this position is because no one else wants it." Cynthia's voice tweaks neurotically.

Spotting Gear's coat on the hook, Cynthia reaches for it, but Jon supersedes. "What do you want with this?"

"I figure I'll just use his truck, since he won't be needing it."

Suspicion fills Sheriff Anderson, as he studies the raging face in front of him. "And why won't Gear be needing his truck?"

"Golly, you're dumb. You just said yourself that he's busy, so why will he need his truck? Geeze."

"Cynthia, just leave. When it gets light out I'll have the guys dig your jeep out, but until then, there's really nothing I can do." What a miserable little woman, Jon thinks to himself.

Glancing down at the floor, Cynthia bends over and picks up a couple ringlets of cereal. Shaking them in her hand, she asks sarcastically. "So, is this your breakfast?"

"Yes, I must've dropped them earlier while I was eating."

"You know, these things can kill you."

"Now a days, what can't?" Jon watches as Cynthia transforms into another change. Her whole body loosens, and she almost appears soft. Jon feels a little sorry for her. "Listen, Cynthia, come back later, okay. I'm very busy." He returns to behind his desk. "I'll send someone for you after we dig out, okay? Are you still staying at your mom's?"

"Yes," she lied. "But, I'll just return in an hour or two."

Leaning back in his chair, he glances out the window and sees pink rising in the eastern sky, dazzling the virgin snow, while tantalizing Jon. His heart skips a beat from the beauty.

Unaware of Cynthia sneaking past him, Jon's too late as she dashes to the back. He rushes at her, cursing her name. "Damn-it, Cynthia. Don't go out there." But his words go unheard, and the tiny woman rambles through the door.

"I'm going to use Gear's truck." She demands, stepping outside.

The sun pierces the sky, filtering through the naked barren trees, bouncing off the snow capped country side, making everything dazzling bright. Jon's eyes are still sensitive from the dark night, and can't reach Cynthia before she discovers Gear's body, the blanket having blown off. Standing there motionless, while gawking at the frozen torso, she asks.

"Is he dead?" Her voice is steady, and a little creepy.

"Yes."

"How?"

"I don't know. I found him lying on the floor when I came back last night. It might have been a heart attack or aneurysm. I won't know until the coroner's office can get here, and that might take some time, that's why he's out here."

"But he's so young." She stares at him queerly. Her voice void of any emotion.

"Yeah, that's what makes it even more sad." Bending over, Jon covers Gear again with the blanket, but this time making sure it's secured. Reaching for Cynthia's arm, he suggested. "Come on, it's cold out here, let's go in."

"No, Sheriff, I really should be going."

Checking his watch, he realizes Deputy Pickens won't arrive for another hour. Jon has an idea, though. "Hey, listen, Cynthia. Why don't you stay here in case the radio comes back on, so I can go home for about an hour. Then, when I get back, I'll dig you out. The roads aren't going to be passable for awhile, so what do you have to lose?"

Cynthia's jaw drops, he can't be serious. Her, of all people! "You know Sheriff, that does sound like a good idea. I'm not tired at all, so why don't you go ahead and do that."

Even though Jon's a little uneasy about leaving her here, he needs to shower, and get out of the office where he's beginning to feel a little cabin feverish. "Good then, I won't be long. If by chance the radio does come on, just tell them to send a trooper up here on the double, okay?"

"Yeah, sure." She sits down in his chair behind the desk

and starts fumbling with some papers.

Jon moves over to the desk and shuffles them together, tossing them on top of the file cabinet. "I'd appreciate it if you wouldn't touch anything."

"Don't worry, I won't." She barks at him, her moods flipping back and forth.

Bolting out the door, Jon slides to the ski-doo. The snow crunches hard, as the crisp frozen air ices his nose hairs. It has to be at least thirty below, he shivers, mounting the sled. Cynthia's crazy if she thinks she'll make it to the Mini-Apple today.

A bright spray of sunlight stabs Candy Jane in the eyes, waking her. At first she's disoriented, but then her senses slowly ease back, as Stray jumps up on her stomach, and begins padding her midsection, putting pressure on her full bladder.

Picking up the cat, she places her on the floor. "Sorry, baby, maybe I'll have time to give you a little loving later." Throughout her whole life, animals have always been attracted to Candy Jane. She figures her scent probably smells like some kind of food they like.

Whipping her legs over the side of the bed, she races into the living room, where she finds Jimmy rolling his head back and forth while moaning.

"Do you think you can keep it down a little bit, Candy. You don't have to walk so loudly."

Jumping onto the couch, she sarcastically asks. "What's wrong, gotta headache?"

"Hah, very funny, Jerry Lewis." Jimmy lunges forward, and standing, staggers to the kitchen. "I need a beer, it's the only thing that's gonna make me feel better."

"My gosh, Jimmy, you're still drunk. Do you think that's a good idea?"

"Yes." He disappears and then returns with two Buds, offering one to Candy, but she refuses. "Whatever!" He plops down on the couch, and twisting the bottle open, downs the brew in three gulps. Opening the other one immediately. "No sense in letting this one get warm." He announces.

Candy's experienced Jimmy's drinking before; seen him go on one of his binges, but this time is different, this time seems fatal.

"Hey, you all right? You've certainly been drinking a lot."

"I'm fine." He spits. "Just tired of this rinky-dink town, and it's rinky-dick mentality."

"Ohhhkay." Candy replies, deciding to see if she can find some coffee to make.

"Hey, I'm sorry," he whispers. "I guess things are just getting to me."

"I don't think drinking is going to help."

"It hasn't hurt so far." He follows Candy into the kitchen, and sits down at the table.

"Do you remember anything about last night?"

"No. Did I do something bad?"

"Not while I was here." She studies her long time friend. "Do you recall the cat?"

"What cat?"

"I found a stray outside last night and brought her in. The two of you were playing all night until you passed out."

"You're crazy, you know how I hate cats."

"Well, you took a shining to this one. She's in your bed right now, snoozing." Candy chuckles, as Jimmy races out of the kitchen and then returns immediately, a look of disbelief on his face.

"I can't believe you brought than scrawny thing into my house. We'll never get rid of it."

"There's no *we* in this." She giggles again.

"This isn't funny, Candy Jane. I want it gone."

"Calm down Jimmy, it's no big deal. After the weather has settled down, I'll take Stray to the pound."

"*Stray*? You named it *Stray*?"

"Yes, I found it appropriate." Candy relaxes, as she tries to think of something other than her predicament. "You're a shit-head, sometimes. You know that?"

"That's calling the kettle black."

Jimmy gets up for his third beer. "So, what are you doing here? Why aren't you at home, where you're supposed to be?"

"I don't know. I stopped by last night, and it was late, you were passed out, so I decided to stay. I didn't think you'd have a problem with that?"

"No, that's fine. You know you're always more than welcome, unless of course, I have company." He winks at her.

"Yeah, right." Candy shakes her head at his insinuation.

Stray suddenly appears in the kitchen, meowing hungrily. Sauntering over to Candy Jane, the feline rubs against her leg, looking desperate and forlorn. Bending over, she picks up the cat and gently begins to pet her.

"I bet you're famished, aren't you." Standing, she continues. "Let's see what this *pig* has to eat."

"Hey, I resent that remark. And please, don't give that fur-ball the wrong first impression of me, I can do that all on my own." Jimmy's acting like he's already buzzed.

More or less ignoring him, Candy opens up a cupboard door and finds a can of tuna fish on the top shelf. Stray meows again.

"Oh, so you can read?" She nuzzles her nose in the soft fur.

"Tell me if I'm wrong, but I think the two of you are falling in love."

"Don't be ridicules, there's only one cat for me, and she's at home, probably mad as hell." She sets the kitten down. "Don't take it personal, Stray."

Dishing the canned fish onto a saucer, Candy places the meal on the floor. The cat bounds to the plate, and after sniffing and recognizing the scent, begins devouring the food.

"Okay, times up. You gonna tell me, or not?" Jimmy's voice breaks the slurping sounds of Stray.

"Tell you what?"

"What happened with Billy. You've been avoiding the subject all morning, and I've had enough. Spill."

Candy's stomach flips. "Nothing really happened." She hands Jimmy his coffee. "I got there late and didn't have time to talk to him. Then the weather started to get bad again, and I had to leave."

Jimmy raises his hands in the air. "Oh, my gosh, stop. So, you didn't break up with him?"

"No, not really, but believe me, you, it's over." Candy's voice softens.

"You're pretty upset, aren't you?"

"To be honest, I just want it to end. I guess when I finally tell him, then it will be over." Candy envisions Billy's body on the couch, and takes a sip of coffee. "Hey, I think I'm going to head home. If my phone is working, I'll call Sven and find out if he's gonna open."

"Well, I don't want to know. I'm taking my receiver off the hook, and if I never get the message, then I don't have to go in."

"Yes, but then I'll tell Toth the truth." Candy Jane tries to joke around as she becomes a little dizzy. Shaking her head, she puts her coat on.

Jimmy watches his best friend sway as she rises. He reaches out for her. "Are you okay? I'm the one who should be wobbling."

She swipes his hand off her arm. "I'm fine. I'm just under a lot of stress right now, and believe a long soothing shower and a good night's sleep will be the cure."

"You don't seem fine to me. Why don't you just hang out here? You can use my bathroom, and sleep in my bed, promise, I won't disturb you."

"No, thanks anyway, Jimmy, but I need to go home."

"Are you taking the cat?"

"No, she's staying here. Later on, we'll put up flyers around the neighborhood, I'm sure there's someone looking for her." Candy puts her hand on the door knob and twists. "I'll see you." Waving, she dashes out the door, a little anxious to get out of the claustrophobic apartment.

"Bye!" She hears his voice trail off.

Trudging through the newly fallen snow, Candy's thankful for Jimmy's car port. It will save her a lot of time not having to clean her car off. Getting in, she starts the sleeping motor, and not letting it warm up enough, puts the cold engine into gear, and grudgingly, Ruby putters down the driveway. The glassy snow cracking beneath the weight.

Turning onto Main Street, Candy Jane drives toward her house, not noticing the sheriff's ski-doo whizzing behind the mounds of snow, as she crawls through the dawns light.

❋　❋　❋

Jon Anderson tears out of his driveway, frustrated by how his wife is treating him. He can't believe Carol's giving him a hard time about being out all night, and not contacting her. She says she's been worried sick; a sign of caring at this point in time, Jon finds hard to believe. He realizes she's using his actions to hold them against him so she doesn't have to be affectionate.

All he wants is a welcome home kiss.

But instead, receives a torrent of accusations, and disheartening assumptions. He's had enough, and stomping upstairs, showers and then bolts out of the house without saying another word to her.

Now, not only is he stressed about these murders, but he's also anxious about his marriage tanking, and to Jon, it feels like it's sinking faster than the Lusitania. For the life of him, he can't figure out what's brought them to this brink. It's as though, one morning Carol woke up and hated his guts.

As Jon ponders, he realizes Carol began acting different right after she joined the Book Club. It was subtle at first, but over time, and especially as of late, she started to become more and more distant.

Seeing a car slowly coming toward him, Jon maneuvers the snow mobile up onto the sidewalk, suddenly hidden behind the mounds of snow. Standing and peering over the piles as the car passes him, Jon recognizes Candy Jane behind the wheel. Recalling his dream from earlier, he wonders if she's been up all night partying and is now just going home?

"Poor woman," he whispers. What she needs is someone to take care of her.

Careening into the Mendelson's driveway, Jon tries to wipe his mind clean of any other thoughts and focus on the task at hand. The best way to do that is to start at square one. With all the excitement last night, he very well could have missed a clue that was right in front of his face.

Crunching up the shoveled wooden steps, Jon's amazed at Mira's perseverance. He can't think of any other woman having just lost a child, going outside and clearing the stairs and walkway. Maybe it's her way of coping with her son's death.

The scene with Carol keeps replaying in his mind, even though he tries to turn off the reel-to-reel. Her actually accusing him of having an affair. Even after he told her he'd been working all night on a case. Why is she being so ridicules? He's always been true to his vows.

No matter how hard things have been lately.

Rapping on the screen door, Sheriff Anderson turns around, admiring the beauty of the virgin snow tundra. The sun shines yellow on the scar-less white, sparkling like a lake of honey.

"Jon?"

Mira's voice makes him jump, as he whips around.

"Morning, Mira. How are you today?"

"I've had better times."

"May I come in."

"Oh, yes, of course, you don't even have to ask." Stepping aside to let him through.

"I just thought I'd come by and see if I missed anything last night. The lights better now, so maybe I'll find something else."

"Do whatever you need to do, Jon."

Studying the stricken woman, he notices that aside from her eyes being swollen and puffy, she seems composed and present.

"You seem to be handling things very well, Mira." He touches her arm as he walks past her, continuing into the living room.

"You don't see me when I'm alone, Jon. This is just a front." She answers softly.

"Still. You're a strong woman, Mira." Sheriff Anderson stands in the middle of the parlor, trying to see anything out of place. Mira comes up behind him. "Did you do anything in here?"

"No, Jon, you told me to stay out, and I did."

Removing his mittens and hat, Jon stuffs them into his parka pockets. Snapping a pair of latex gloves on, he carefully begins searching for hidden clues. Glancing down at the carpet, he notices there are Fruit Loops everywhere. Something he didn't see last night. It's as if the person eating them started to panic, and began flailing them around the room.

Suddenly, Jon deduces that there must have been someone else here yesterday afternoon before Mira got home. Someone who might have witnessed everything, and is now in danger themselves.

"Mira!" Jon calls out.

"Yes, Jon." He hears from the back of the house, and waits for her to appear.

"Mira, did you say Candy Jane came by yesterday?"

"I don't know for sure, but I gathered she did."

"Do you recall her ever eating Fruit Loops?"

"I couldn't tell you Jon. I never really visited with her for long. She and Billy would disappear into his bedroom when I was around. It seemed like Billy might have been embarrassed by me."

"I'm sure that wasn't the case Mira. Don't be so hard on yourself, okay?"

Jon reevaluates the MO for the murders, and sees a pattern. This guy is not the *snapped-a-brain-cell kind of killer*, but a plotting and scheming murderer, the kind that really scares him.

Static noise wrinkles in the air, snapping Jon's nerves in the peace and quiet. Turning to reach for the walkie-talkie on the coffee table, he smacks his knee against the marble edged mesa. Hobbling back, he accidentally falls onto the coach. Lifting the black box to his mouth, he moans. "Cynthia?"

"Yes, hey Sheriff, how did you know it's me? You okay?"

"Yeah, yeah. What is it?"

"I wanted to let you know that I got hold of the State Troopers."

"You did? How?" Jon had checked the radio himself, and there was no getting through.

"My cell is receiving service, now, so the first thing I did was call St. Paul. They're sending a unit immediately."

A sense of relief fills Jon as he reaches his hand in between the cushions without even thinking. A small poke sticks the tip of his finger, and carefully pulling the chasm apart, Jon looks into the crevasse. A shiny rhinestone brioche sparkles back at him. "Cynthia, I'm gonna have to call you back. Don't go anywhere."

"But Sheriff."

Turning the receiver off, he fumbles for a plastic baggie.

Sliding the toy jewelry into the evidence pouch, Jon examines the piece more carefully. It looks like something a child would wear.

Mira, returning, stares at him questioningly. "Jon, everything okay? You don't look so good."

"No, I'm fine, I'm just a little tired, and I slammed my knee a couple minutes ago." He quiets for a moment. "Hey, Mira, have you had any children over here, lately?"

"Not a one, Jon. Why?"

"No reason."

White noise fills the air again. "Sheriff, hey Sheriff, it's me."

Standing, and hearing his knee click, he limps out of the crime scene, and over to the bay window. The day is warming as Jon notices tiny drops of silver water melting away from the stalactite icicles hanging from snow capped eves.

"What is it, Cynthia? I told you I'd call you back."

"I know, Sheriff," her voice stiffens. "But I had to tell you that Mark is on his way over, and I'm wondering if you're still going to help me with the jeep?"

"It'll get done, Cynthia. Right now, I'm in the middle of something very important, can't you wait."

"Are you reneging on our deal?"

"No." Jon hears an edginess in Cynthia's voice. "I just can't do it right this minute. Plus, it'd really help a lot if you could just hang out for a little while longer."

Cynthia doesn't know what to think. Seldom, if ever, has someone told her she's needed. Her heart swells with admiration, and she chokes out. "Okay, I'll stay for a little while longer, but then I'm outta here."

"Thanks, Cynthia." Jon hoping he sounds sincere. "I've gotta go now."

"No, wait, Sheriff, I forgot to tell you about last night."

"What about it."

"Well, I'm not sure if this is important to you or not, but I saw Candy Jane Cane leaving Toth's house. I thought it rather odd since they hate each other."

"What do you know about Toth's?"

"Nothing, I was just driving by, and saw her running out the back, that's all."

"Well, just mind your own business. Ten-four?"

"Ten-four."

So, he has a witness that places Candy Jane at Toth's house, too. More and more evidence is pointing toward her, and Sheriff Anderson knows he has to find Candy and question her before she skips town.

Sheriff Anderson hears the front door open and close and wonders how he's going to break the news about Gear's death to Mark, his one and only deputy, now.

6

Candy Jane races to her house as fast as she can, which is at a snail's pace. The roads are still pretty bad, even though they've been plowed and salted. She prays that Sven will open today so she can stay busy, hopefully taking her mind off of the situation.

Daylight's beginning warmth pierces the coldness she's been feeling, and for the first time in a couple of days, Candy Jane actually feels kind of good. Pulling into her driveway, and making a mental note to herself to give her handy-boy a bonus for staying on top of this snowstorm, she drives into the garage, and turns off the car.

Instantly, she hears Amelia meowing at the door. Her loud pleas makes Candy's heart sink. Guilt rips at her, and that brief feeling of well being quickly disappeared. Feeling a cold tear roll down her cheek, Candy wipes it away and studies the solidifying drop on her finger. It reminds her of a breast implant. Little bags of goo.

Amelia is not a happy camper, as Candy opens the door, the cries become louder. Hurriedly, she fills the empty bowl with some dry cat food, and sets down a tiny saucer of milk, a rare treat for the feline. There's one last cant, and the cat retires to her dish, content in getting the last word in.

Surveying her house, Candy realizes how disgusting the dwelling is. The sink is full of dirty plates and glasses, and there's a rancid stench of used kitty litter in the air. What has she been doing with her time to let her home get so out of control?

The phone wails, and Candy Jane picks it up before it rings again. She has a splitting headache, and wonders if maybe she should just call in sick tonight.

"Hello." She grumbles.

"Candy Jane, is that you?"

"Yes." She pauses for a moment. "Candy, it's me, Patricia."

Not recognizing the voice, it takes an instant before Candy realizes who she's talking to. "Oh, yes, Patricia, you sound totally different on the phone. Hey, I was just going to call to see if Sven's opening today."

"He is, but not 'till a little later, and only for dinner."

"So, I have to come in?" Part of her wants the Swiss to say, *no*.

"Yeah, I'm sorry. We can't get hold of a lot of people. Your phone seems to be the only one working."

"Lucky me!" Her voice is laced with irritation. "What

time?" Glancing up at the clock, she sees that it's already twelve thirty.

"As soon as you can."

"But I thought we're only opening for dinner."

"You might be working alone, so there's a lot of set up."

Candy feels like she's going to blow a gasket. She should cruise by Jimmy's and pick the boozer up, drunk or not. "Fine!" Candy doesn't mean to snap. "I'm sorry. I'll be there when I can."

Hanging up the phone, Candy Jane has an urge for a drink, but then decides against it, figuring it will be best for her if she stays sober right now. Keep her head clear, it'll be easier to stay in the moment. The thought puts her a little at ease, but not much.

There are still three dead men!

Maybe she should call the sheriff, get all of this off her chest. She was just in the wrong place at the wrong time. Three times for that matter. Candy chuckles, feeling herself becoming a little giddy as tension begins to nibble on her nerves.

Knowing she's delaying the inevitable, she strolls to her bedroom to freshen up. Her uniform is still clean, although a little wrinkled, but what difference does it make? She's probably going to be the only server there, along with Patricia, and Toth. Suddenly remembering Hector's demise, Candy shivers.

Nauseous tidal waves cross her; flashes like a broken movie reel zip through her brain. For a moment, Candy believes she's going to pass out, and quickly sits down on the bed.

She can't do this. She has to tell someone, these events are eating at her like a turkey vulture on the road kill. What she should do is go into work, and call Sheriff Anderson from there. Hopefully arrange to meet him after her shift.

Heading to her car, Candy Jane flings herself into the vehicle, and turns toward Sven's. She sees someone on a snow mobile coming toward her, but can't make out the figure. As they got closer, the rider disappears behind a mountain of snow. Just someone out enjoying the beauty, Candy thinks, wondering if she'll ever experience that pleasure again.

Arriving at the empty parking lot at Sven's, Candy veers her vehicle toward the back, thankful that the plows have already cleared the driveway. The only other cars there are Patricia's and Jesus' Terino.

Breathing deeply, Candy reaches under her seat for the now frozen apron. She contemplates the frostbitten stains, and wonders if they'll start to smell after thawing.

"Oh, the things a person thinks of when on the verge of insanity." She whispers to herself, as she gates toward the door.

Maybe she should call Billy's house later and ask for him. Act as though there's nothing wrong, like everything is normal, distract her scent from the scenes, maybe that's a good idea?

Reaching for the ice crusted handle and opening the steel door, a dank staleness greets her in the dim lit hallway. Silence bounces from wall to wall. It reminds her of the *Shin-*

ing. Chills ripple her chapped shins.

Trouncing through the kitchen and into the main dining room, Candy Jane hears clanking echoing from the lounge. Poking her head around the corner, she doesn't see anyone, until Patricia, rising from behind the bar, shrieks in fright, almost dropping the six pack of beer she is stocking.

"Oh, Candy, damn, you scared the hell out of me. I wasn't expecting anyone this early."

"You told me to come in right away to set up, remember."

"I didn't think you'd rush. Toth isn't even here, yet."

"So, you talked to him?"

"No, I left a message on his phone, why?"

"I just wanted to ask him something about the schedule."

"Planning on taking a vacation?"

Patricia is being kind of weird, asking her all these question. Or maybe, Candy is just being paranoid. "I wish." She turns back toward the dining room. "I guess I'll get started while I'm here."

Lifting the chairs off the tables, Candy Jane is soothed by the humming ice machine and refrigerator. Familiar sounds, ones she has found comfort in over the years of being alone, because when she really thinks about it, there is no one out there who she can call a best friend.

The couple of relationships she's had in her life, were meaningless, and even though she considers Jimmy to be a good buddy, he's not her confidant. And right at this point she can take him or leave him.

Finishing, Candy sits down for a minute in the darkness,

rubbing her face with her hand. She can't seem to shake this sensation of strangeness out of her system. What did all three men have in common? Billy and Toth hated each other, but that was because of her. And Gear, well everyone knew Gear, and there are very few women left in Mongoose Falls who haven't known him on a personal level. He was sort of a player, but his game never interested Candy Jane.

"Hey, quit sitting on your ass, and get to work." For a moment Candy thinks it's Toth screaming at her, but then looking toward the splinter of light coming from the kitchen, she sees it's Jimmy.

Candy wishes she would've taken Toth's pulse before she left, because now, she's not positive if he really is dead. She just assumed he was because of how hard his head hit the floor. What if he is alive and he shows up?

Frogs begin to jump in her gut.

"What are you doing here?"

"Well, when Patricia called my house and told me that she didn't think you could handle working alone tonight, I figured I'd come in and save your sorry behind."

"Thanks, but no thanks. Either you go, or I will."

"What do you mean? I didn't drive all the way out here, just to turn around and go back."

"Fine, then I'll leave."

"Why are your panties in such a twist?"

"Shut up, will ya?"

Just then Patricia comes into the room, and looking at Jimmy, says in her Swiss laced accent. "Oh, good, you're here. Thanks for coming in."

"Yeah, sure no problem."

"So, hey Patricia, since Jimmy's here, can I go home. I thought you said that we only needed one person to work today."

"Sven's wants you both here. He's not coming in, and I still don't know where Hector is. So no, I can't let you go, sorry."

"This is ridicules." Candy spits, beginning to get agitated.

"If we're not busy, you can go first, okay." Patricia trying to placate Candy.

"Whatever!" Candy whips around and heads for the bus station, snagging a mini box of Fruit Loops from the counter. She rips the colorful box open and pours a handful into her mouth.

"Maybe you should lay off those things for a while. They're starting to make you crazy." Jimmy suggests. "All that sugar and colored poison."

"Maybe you should mind your own business."

Candy Jane's furious. She doesn't know why she's so mad at Jimmy. He hasn't done anything wrong, except for the fact that the only time she really needed to confide in him, he was blasted.

"*What* is wrong with you?" He screams across the room. "You've been nothing but a bitch to me since I arrived."

"I don't want to be here, and I see no sense in the two of us staying."

"Why don't we wait for Hector to show up, and then he can make a decision."

"Oh, we know how that's going to turn out. He'll make

me stay, and let you go."

"That's because the man's in-loooove with you."

"You're disgusting." Candy giggles slightly, and begins to relax.

"Come on, I know you secretly have a thing for him, too."

Candy suddenly burst into laughter, the stress of the past twenty-four hours finally finding an outlet. "You're so intuitive." She wipes a tear from her lash. "I wish I'd known how psychic you were, I would've employed your services earlier." Holding her aching diaphragm from the sudden explosion of spasms.

"Now, who's being the smart-ass." Jimmy approaches Candy and wraps his arm around her shoulder. "Listen, sweetie, I know things are rough for you right now, but rest assured, you can always find an ear to blab into right here." He points to his left lobe.

"Thanks, Jimmy, I appreciate that." She wants to include, that he's always too drunk to pay attention to what she has to say, but doesn't want to dredge up another argument.

"And trust me," Jimmy continues with his promises, sounding like a lame politician. "I'll make sure I get you out of this dump, and on your way home as soon as I'm able."

Candy half expects him to finish with a *vote for me* plea. "If it happens, then it happens. If not, I'm fine staying. I guess my blood sugar must be jumping off the roof."

"It's because you're addicted to that crappy cereal."

Opening her hand, Candy realizes that she's been holding some in her palm, all crushed and reduced to powder. "Maybe you're right."

"I know I'm right."

"Whatever you say, James." Candy removes his arm and reaches for a towel. Come on, we should get started."

"I'm going to go get a cup of coffee first. I think there's some in the bar." He disappears though the beaded doorway.

Candy suspects he's going to beg a drink off of Patricia, and that will form the course for the night. And if Patricia refuses, he'll order one, pretending it's for a customer, and drink it himself. Some nights Jimmy drank so much in one shift that he barely walked out with any tips. And tonight had all the characteristics of one of those evenings.

Deciding it isn't doing her any good to gloat about his behavior, Candy Jane begins wiping the tables, and setting them. She still hasn't turned on the lights, and the soft white grayness of the air calms her.

Lost in her thoughts, Candy jumps when she hears, "Hey, Candy Cane, my Christmas Candy Cane." For an instant, she thinks it's Billy, and her heart begins to beat out of control.

Realizing its Jimmy, Candy screams. "Damn-it, Jimmy, you know how I hate that."

Throwing the wet dirty towel at him, she pegs him in the head, tussling his hair.

He begins chuckling, and runs after her. Candy dodges around the chairs, but he catches her, and lifting her in the air, spins her around.

"Let me down, you moron." Candy orders. "What is wrong with you?"

He lets her slide down his body, and then says. "Patricia can't get hold of Toth. She thinks something might be wrong because this is so unlike him."

Candy can picture the blood draining from her face, and is glad the room is still dim, otherwise Jimmy might notice her pallor. "I'm sure he'll be here. This job is the most important thing Hector has in his life."

"Besides, you!" Jimmy bends over and howls. "Gosh, I crack myself up sometimes."

"You and only you." Candy pictures Toth lying naked on the hard wood floor, dead by her hands. "Are we still opening?"

"I guess, so. Patricia called Sven and he told her to take over the managing position until Toth arrives." Jimmy scans the ear shot area and leans in closer to Candy. "Personally, I think that Sven has been training Patricia all along to take over Toth's job."

"Why?"

"Why? How can you even ask that? He's an ass-hole. Everybody hates him, even the customers. I think Sven is beginning to see him as a determent to the business."

"Ah, whatever. I don't really care. I just want to get this night over with, and go home."

"Hey, you two." They both turn and watch as Patricia saunters toward them, rolling into her coat. "Sven wants me to go over to Toth's and make sure everything is all right. I won't be long."

Startled that Patricia will discover the body, she reaches for her arm, stopping her. "Do you really think that's necessary? After all, he is a very responsible man, and I'm sure it's the roads that are making him late."

"Yeah, Patricia, he'll be here. It's just taking him longer to swallow his ugly pills today." Jimmy begins laughing again, and Candy senses he's already drunk. "I don't see why you should risk going into a ditch over him." He's on a roll. "Plus, do you know what's going to happen? As soon as you leave, he'll pull up. You wait and watch."

"First, I kind of think Toth is handsome." Patricia chimes. "And second I don't know why you have to be so hard on him. What has he ever done to you?"

"Where should I start?"

"Don't start anywhere." Her voice growing defensive. "If the opportunity ever arouse for me and Hector to go out, I'd jump at the chance."

"That's nice Patricia." Suddenly losing a little bit of respect for the Swiss woman, Candy *now* wishes she would go over to his house and find his dead body.

"I still don't think it's a good idea if you pop-in on Toth. What if he has a hooker there, it could be very embarrassing for the both of you." Jimmy won't let it go.

"He's not like that."

"Oh, little do you know. Right, Candy?" He nudges her with his elbow.

"Hey, leave me out of this. I don't care what happens, just do it, or not." She side-steps away from Jimmy. "But, maybe he's right. I really don't see the point. He'll either show up, or not. My bet is that he'll be here." Maybe it's best that Toth stay undiscovered for a little while longer.

Patricia begins to shake her coat off. "I think you two are right. If he doesn't appear, then we'll just run the show without him. I'm sure we'll have no problem."

Candy Jane is amazed at how good Patricia's English is for the short time that she's lived in Mongoose Falls. She wonders what ever brought her here in the first place, and Candy realizes, she knows nothing about the woman.

Enveloping Candy with his ape arm, Jimmy reassures. "Me and Candy, here, we can handle just about anything you throw at us. Right, chum?" He squeezes her close to him.

"Get off me, you slug." She pushes him away, putting a little more force into the shove than she intends. Jimmy falls back against a table, and almost tips it over.

Straightening himself out. "Gosh, you don't have to play butch with me. What's with you tonight?"

"Just leave me alone." Candy warns.

Patricia has since returned to the office after putting out the open sign, and Candy stands in the dimming evening light. Any minute now the doors might be bombarded with hungry families, demanding service on the run, slovenly shoveling food onto their plates, just to end up wasting half of it.

"Pigs." She hisses.

"What?"

"Oh, nothing. Just ignore me, Jimmy. I'm in a foul mood and I don't think there's anything that will help it."

"How about a little green bud?" Jimmy twirls a joint between his fingers.

"No, I don't think so, I'd hate to waste a good high on this place."

"Then let's go get a drink."

"No! What's it going to take for you to see that I want to stay sober today."

"All right, all ready." Jimmy stares at his friend. "Are you gonna tell me what's wrong?"

Candy places her hand on his cheek, feeling the slight stubble from his unshaven face. "Trying to grow a beard?" She asks, attempting to ease the strain and change the subject.

"No, it's just a look." Jimmy tilts his nose in the air. "And what do you care, anyways? Something's wrong and you won't share it with me."

"Listen, Jimmy, for the last time, there's nothing wrong. I just feel a little under the weather."

"Yeah, right." He stares at her through blank eyes, salutes, then turns and walks away.

What a drama queen, Candy thinks, knowing she hasn't heard the last of it. He'll start up again in an hour or so, snorting around like a lost dog. She'll not give in, though. If no one knows she was at Toth's last night, they can never connect her to the murder.

The sucking sound of the revolving door brings Candy Jane to attention, as the pale yellow sunlight pierces the room. Twelve people trounce in, stomping their feet free of snow as they shake flakes from their coats.

"Here we go again." Candy whispers to herself as she gets up to greet them.

❄ ❄ ❄

Patricia Moldine sneers as she watches Jimmy and Candy greet the incoming customers. What do they know about love? Toth is a unique specimen when it comes to being a potential lover. Strong, unwilling to give in to the petty demands of his lessers. They have a lot in common, too bad he has a thing for that skank, Cynthia and Candy.

She can understand why he'd be attracted to Candy. In a way she is cute, but not really a beauty. She's nice, but in a hillbilly sort of way, Patricia thinks, retreating back to the office.

Right now though, the most important thing, is nobody finding out who she really is. If that were to happen, all the suspicion will fall on her. And then one call to Interpol and her life in Mongoose Falls will be over.

Closing the door behind her, Patricia wipes her brow with a bar towel, and plops down in the desk chair. And if there's one thing she knows for certain, she'll stop at no lengths to secure her freedom.

Just ask her late husband.

❄ ❄ ❄

Carol Anderson steps out of the shower still feeling a chill even after blasting herself with hot jets of water. She hates the cold, the snow, everything about Mongoose Falls. Except for Jon, but even those feelings are waning, and she wonders if she's falling out of love with her husband?

The once hot and uncontrollable passion between them is nothing more than a flicker off an old match, now. They really don't have much in common, he with his police work, and she with her book club. They couldn't be more different. They're more like room-mates than lovers. Carol can't pinpoint the day things began to change. She just stopped being sexually attracted to him. Deep down Carol feels lonely and distraught; like something is out there and she's missing it.

Turning the flame down below the tea pot, Carol leans against the stove for a minute, trying to warm her butt. This weather is making her bonkers; having been cramped up in this house all winter.

For twenty-five years it's been her home. Redecorating several times, but it always seems to look the same. Her mind scrambles when she tries to conjure up the reasons why they never moved to California like they planned when she and Jon first got married.

The biggest thing was when Jon got elected sheriff. Little did they know at the time that it would be the spike that would keep Carol from living her dream.

Carol's never been one for making friends. She attends parties and benefits, but has never desired a best buddy, or for that matter, a casual one. Recently though, her and Mira have started talking again, and Carol hopes to have dinner with her at some point. Try to reconnect from their past.

By the looks of it though, that some point is a long time

away.

Suddenly, Carol decides the neighborly thing to do would be to pay her respects to Mira, offer her condolences. Maybe take her a treat or something. Warming, as her blood begins to tingle, Carol gently places the chocolate cake she baked for Jon in a Tupperware container, figuring she can always bake him another one later.

Dressing, Carol skips out of the kitchen, and thinks about writing Jon a note, but figures she'll run into him at the Mendelson's. Her mood seems a little lighter, and she's not sure if it's because she's getting out of the house, or because she's going to see Mira.

Trying to recall what happened between them back in high school that ended their friendship, Carol's memory can't resurrect the reason. Probably an over-hormonal episode about some boy, or something so minor they could've worked it out. But then Mira's family uprooted on a whim, and Carol hasn't seen her until joining the book club a year ago. She didn't even know Mira had been living in Mongoose Falls for the past two decades, until then. And it was as though they'd never fought. Their friendship rekindling immediately.

She returned with a son, and husband, but then he had a fatal accident and Mira inherited a small fortune. But she never speaks of those things, her privacy is impenetrable. Then the Club formed, and when Carol saw Mira across the room she felt as though her life had opened up again. Her brain began to function on a different level, new sensations flowed through her like hot molten lava. She can't explain any of it. All she knows is that she likes it.

Carefully easing out of the garage, Carol Anderson drives down the plowed street, the shining sun beating off the bright white, blinding her for a moment. Rubbing her eyes, Carol sees blue sparkles in front of her, and slows down, not wanting to lose control.

Sheriff Jon Anderson speeds across the frozen bog toward Toth's house, praying that word hasn't gotten out about the murders yet. He knows how fast the news will travel, and by the time it gets back to him the whole story will be different.

Jon wonders why he hasn't heard anything from the Troopers, yet. He thought they'd be here by now, at least that's the impression Cynthia gave. Looking at his watch, he realizes it's close to three, as worry begins to etch its way through his spine.

Pulling in front of Hectors house, Jon dismounts the mobile and studies the perimeter. Everything seems to be the same as he left it.

Yanking his handkerchief out of his pocket, Jon covers his mouth and nose, as he steps into the dark kitchen. He can still see his billowing breath hanging in the air as he crosses into the dining room, and studying the covered hump laying by the table, Jon decides to let the coroner's office deal with the body. He needs to focus on the crime scene, try to discover something new now that his nerves have calmed down.

Untangling the flashlight from his belt, he roves it around, intrigued by the closed door down the hall. He didn't notice that last night while he was here. Slowly easing himself along the wall, Jon tries not to make any noise, not wanting to scare off anyone who might be here.

Bracing himself, Jon draws his gun, and aiming it at the portal, raises his leg and kicks the plywood door. His foot drives right threw it, and angrily, and a little embarrassed, he yanks it out. Reaching for the knob, which he should have done in the first place, he finds the handle unlocked.

"Good job, Dick Tracey." Jon whispers to himself, thankful no one is here to see his bumbling performance.

Still holding his gun aimed, Jon searches the wall for a switch, and finding one, fills the dark room with a pink, pale light. The place is a pit, and if there's someone hiding in here, the only way out is through Jon. Removing a gray shade from the window, he's suddenly blinded as sunlight pierces his eyes like a needle through a hole.

None of this makes sense.

Who would take a chance and come out all this way, in last night's weather, just to murder Toth?

Was it, Candy Jane?

A small connection begins to appear as he clearly sees why Toth and Billy are victims, but where does Gear come in? Maybe he's just a random killing. Maybe his deputy saw something he wasn't supposed to see and had to murder him, as well.

Meandering out onto the porch, Jon gazes over the frozen prairie, chalk white, glistening drifts edge the horizon. Out of the corner of his eye he thinks he sees a sparkle, and jumping over the railing, trudges over to the garbage barrel to investigate.

Glancing over the rim, he sees a layer of snow covering the half burnt contents. It looks like whatever was being burned was extinguished by the blizzard. Clearing some of the ice away, Jon pulls out a charred scarf, and notices the babushka has the same design of jewelry as the broach he found earlier. If he can locate the owner, he'll find the murderer.

Growing excited, Jon closes up the house and hops on the sled. He has to get to Sven's and have a little chat with Miss Cane. Maybe it was a love triangle crime. Both men wanting her, but she not really desiring either of them. She is quite cute, and he can empathize with the men's turmoil. Maybe Candy Jane just got fed up with it, and decided to put an end to the nonsense.

Whatever the reason, he now has a prime suspect.

Jimmy is the first to notice the sheriff wheel through the revolving door. He playfully saunters up to him, and wraps his arm around the officer as if they had been friends for years.

"Why, hello, Sheriff Anderson! What brings you out this way." Jimmy is apparently drunk, but he himself, does not realize it.

Jon will deal with him later.

"I just want to get a late lunch." He replies, feeling a little awkward as he pushes Jimmy away.

Taking offense, Jimmy splays his arm through the air, directing Jon to a table. "Right this way, *Sheriff*."

Following the toasted Twinkie, Jon shakes his head, thinking maybe it's time Jimmy went to rehab before he hurts somebody. Stopping in front of a table, Jimmy turns toward Jon, and with a stern voice, announces. "There you are, *Sir*." And pouting, asks. "Can I get you something to drink?"

"Coffee will be great Jimmy. And hey, don't take anything personal, okay. I just don't like being touched."

"I'll have to remember that, Jon." Jimmy feels a special warmth for the kind hearted sheriff, who on several occasions defended him from the gay basher's verbal and sometimes physical abuse. There hasn't been an incident in quite a while, and Jimmy has Jon Anderson to thank for that.

Before Jimmy leaves the table, Jon inquires. "Is Candy Jane here?"

"Yes, she is." Jimmy seems a little disappointed. "Would you rather have her wait on you?"

"No, Jimmy." Jon watches as his face transforms into a disappointed little boy's. "I just need to ask her a couple of questions. That's all."

"You gonna ask her out? You know she's a free woman now. She just broke up with that slug Billy Mendelson, so she's ripe for the picken'." Jimmy winks. "If you get my drift."

Even though Jon knows Jimmy's joking, it kind of pisses him off. "You know perfectly well that I'm married."

"Hey, I didn't mean anything by it. I'm just messin' with you." Jimmy turns to leave, adding. "Things must be really good between you and the Missus."

Jon sat there contemplating what Jimmy just said about Candy Jane breaking up with Billy. Did she fall in-love with Toth, and Billy gave her a hard time about ending their relationship, so she resorted to killing him. Then, Toth dumped her, so she murdered him, too?

Are the answers that easy?

"Sheriff, did you want to see me?" Candy Jane sets his coffee down in front of him.

Her demeanor cool and collected.

Looking up at her, Jon is caught a little off guard. Her blue eyes meet his, and for a brief instant, for reasons unbeknownst to him, he yearns for her.

"Um, yes." He motions for her to have a seat. "Do you have a minute to talk? There are a few questions I need to ask you."

"I'm pretty busy, can this wait?"

Jon glances around the empty dining room. "No, not really."

"What's this about?"

"It's concerning Billy Mendelson."

"What about him?"

"When is the last time you saw him?"

"The day before yesterday?"

"So, you weren't at his house yesterday?"

"Yes, I was. I stopped by before work. We were supposed to meet, but when I got there, and he never answered, I left." She shuffles her feet. "Why?"

"Oh, no reason." Jon scribbles something in his notebook. "You didn't find it odd that he didn't answer?"

"Well, I figured he was mad at me because I was forty-five minutes late. I was going to call him from work, but the phones were all down, and today, well, I just haven't had time. But maybe I'll go do that, now."

"So, you haven't heard?"

"Heard what?"

"Maybe you might want to sit down, Candy."

She studies him oddly, and slides into the booth. "What is it?"

He reaches out and takes her hand, it's soft and creamy. "Candy, Billy's dead."

Her face remains expressionless, as Jon scans it for a sign. "What did you just say?"

"I said, Billy's dead."

"What do you mean? How?"

"I can't go into details, but he was found at home yesterday by his mom."

"Mira found him? Oh, that poor woman."

Jon's surprised at Candy's reaction, or maybe, lack of reaction. Not even a hint of sorrow. He'd expected her to break down, but she just sat there, blank faced. Maybe his words haven't sunk in yet. Or, she might be in shock.

He releases her hand, his fingers tingle like sparklers.

"So, Candy, are you sure you didn't see him alive yesterday?"

"No, I didn't." Candy feels like she's going to throw up. She doesn't know how to react, or what he's expecting her to say. Suddenly standing, she sways as her legs feel like rubber. "Listen Sheriff, I think the best thing I can do right now, is get back to work. Can we finish this later."

"Why aren't you upset?" Jon wants to shake an answer out of her.

"I guess it really hasn't hit me yet. But when the reality finally sinks in, I'm sure you won't want to be around. We all have our own ways of dealing with things, right?" She's surprising herself at how cold and uncaring she's being. But that's how she feels.

As Candy is about to turn away, Sheriff Anderson touches her arm. "Just one more thing, if you don't mind."

"Sure, Sheriff, but I don't know what else I can tell you."

"Were you at Hector Toth's house last night?"

"Hell, no." Lying. "Why in the world would I go over there?"

"I don't know."

"If you don't believe me, ask him yourself. He should be here any minute."

"So, he's late?"

"Yeah, nobody has seen him or heard from him. It's kind of weird because he's such a stickler about punctuality."

Jon doesn't take his eyes off Candy Jane's face. He's searching for a lie to sneak out, somewhere within the premature wrinkles, or a twitch in her pink tempting lips, but there's nothing.

"Maybe I'll go by his house on my way out, see if everything's all right."

"I'm sure Patricia will appreciate that." Candy points toward the bar. "Would you like me to get her?"

"No, that's fine." Jon glances at his watch. "I do have to go though. Can you have Jimmy bring me my check."

Candy waves her hand in the air. "Go ahead, Jon, you know everything's on the house for you and your deputies." Candy Jane chokes on the last word.

"You okay?" He inquires, tossing a dollar bill on the table.

"Yeah, I just swallowed wrong." Candy Jane coughs. "See ya." Turning around, she scurries away.

Jon watches as she pulls a box of Fruit Loops out of her apron pocket, and shakes some into her mouth. He touches the baggie of ringlets and torched scarf in his coat. He thinks about asking Candy if the wrap is hers, but decides it'll be better to wait. He doesn't want to let the cat out of the bag too soon, he snickers, slashing out into the freezing air.

"Sheriff, Sheriff," Jon hears. Looking back, he sees Jimmy running after him, flailing his gloves in the air.

Puffing up to him, Jimmy outstretches his arm and says, "You forgot these, and I'm sure you're going to need them." Jon doesn't know what it is about Jimmy, but it seems that there's always a sexual undertone to everything he says. Maybe that's just how he is.

"Thanks! You'd better get back before you freeze." Jon mounts the ski-doo. "Hey, wait a minute, Jimmy."

The cladly clothed waiter stops in his tracks, and faces

Jon. "Yes?" He asks timidly.

"Do you know where Candy Jane was last night?"

"Yeah, she was at my house."

"What time did she get there?"

"I'd say around six, six-thirty. Why?"

"No reason. And did she stay all night?"

"She left this morning." Jimmy did not want to tell the sheriff that he passed out and doesn't really know if Candy stayed the night, or not. All he knows is that she was there when he woke up this morning. "Why, you thinking about asking her out?"

"Enough of that." Jon's voice becoming perturbed.

"Okay, then, well, thanks for the dollar."

"You're welcome." Jon starts the engine, revving it a little. "See you later, Jimmy." He eases away, and watches as Jimmy scoots back to the warmth.

"Now, what?" Jon says out loud, trying to think of what his next move should be.

Patricia eases the beaded strings back into place, and ducks into the bar shadows as the sheriff glances her way. She'd been keeping an eye on their conversation, and by the looks of it, Sheriff Anderson suspects Candy Jane. Things could not be better, she smiles to herself and floats back to the cooler.

Grabbing a case of *Miller High Life,* she lifts the box without strain, and loads the refrigerators. All she has to do is stay out of the picture, remain disconnected from the whole scene, and then Candy will be arrested, Cynthia will be taken care of, and she, Celeste Robideax, will live happily ever after, without anyone being the wiser.

❋ ❋ ❋

Candy Jane's skin is cold and clammy as she jets into the kitchen. Her stomach gurgles, threatening to upsurge. Running behind the dish station, she bends over and dry heaves into a garbage can, as her body shakes with spasms. Hot tears begin to stream down her face. She has to compose herself. Obviously, Sheriff Anderson speculates something, that's why he's asking all of those questions.

Heat waves wash over her, and believing she is going to faint, pushes open the back door, and rushing outside, leans against the frozen brick building. Her breathing is hurried, as she tries to calm herself down.

"Candy, Candy Jane?"

Hearing Jimmy's muffled voice, she collapses to the ground as he turns the corner.

Dashing over to her, he falls to his knees and wraps his arms around her. "Candy, honey, are you all right?"

"Billy's dead." She starts to cry.

"What?" Jimmy lifts her face toward him. "What did you say?"

"I said, Billy's dead. That's what Sheriff Anderson wanted to tell me." Candy bawls.

"How?"

"He didn't say, but I don't think it was accidental."

"Why, what makes you say that?"

"Just by some of the things he was asking me, they were kind of accusing."

Jimmy recalls his conversation with the sheriff in the parking lot. "Oh, don't be silly. You're being paranoid because of what just happened. I'm sure he's just trying to figure things out. I mean, he was alive when you saw him yesterday, right?"

"I don't know. No one answered the door, so I left."

"So you didn't even see him? You lied to me."

"My gosh, Jimmy, that's not important right now." If anything, Jimmy has a knack for pissing her off just at the right minute, making her forget about everything else she's feeling.

Jimmy stands up and helps Candy to her feet. "Come on, let's get inside before we both catch our deaths."

Candy is reluctant. The last place she wants to go is back into Sven's. Those awful scents of sauerkraut and polish sausages.

All of a sudden, Patricia comes running outside toward them. "Jimmy, Candy, come quick, something has happened to Toth."

Looking at each other, they hurry through the door, and into the welcome warmth. At first it's too hot for Candy Jane and she just wants to go back outside, be by herself, not hear what Patricia is going to say. Candy already knows what the announcement is about.

The Swiss woman is in tears as she leans over the bar

weeping.

Jimmy scampers over to attend her. "Man, what is going on with you women tonight."

"Toth's been killed." Patricia wails.

Candy feels herself sway, and quickly grabs onto the back of a chair.

"He was found on his dining room floor, dead." Patricia's sobs shake her whole body.

She really must've been in love with him, Candy realizes, recalling her unemotional reaction when Sheriff Anderson told her of Billy's demise. No wonder he suspects her.

Joining Jimmy, Candy embraces Patricia, trying to comfort her with generic terms.

"It'll be okay, Patricia, there's a reason for everything. I know it's hard, but time heals all." Now, Candy Jane really feels like throwing up.

Patricia pushes them both away. "Please, thank-you, but I'm sure the two of you could care less about Hector. I know how you talked about him, what you thought of him, and now you expect me to believe your words of sympathy?"

"I said them with sincerity." Candy whip-lashes back, suddenly feeling very angry. "Do they know what happened?"

Patricia gawks at Candy. "I would think you'd be a little more upset after finding out your boyfriend has been murdered, too."

"What are you talking about?"

"They were both killed the same way. Both men had puncture wounds at the cervical, which is the base of the neck." Patricia points to the area. "From the rumors flying around, Fruit Loops were discovered at both crime scenes, so the murderer is being called, *Fruit Loops the Serial Killer*." Patricia's demeanor has calmed down considerably.

"Ha," Jimmy slaps Candy on the shoulder. "You've been eat..." He stops short, side glancing Candy Jane. She widens her eyes, indicating for him to shut up.

"What'd you say?" Patricia inquires.

"Nothing, I was thinking of something else."

Patricia glares at Jimmy, oddly. It's as if her nice personality has vanished, and is replaced with a new, ugly Patricia. Plus, her English has improved drastically within the past half hour. It's as though she doesn't have an accent at all.

Something's not right!

Is Patricia really who she says she is? And how does she know all these details about the murders. Sheriff Anderson certainly didn't inform Candy of any details.

Wiping her sweaty forehead, Candy is relieved that she didn't kill Toth, after all. So, there's nothing to worry about. An unexpected gush of relief rolls over her, as her knees buckle slightly, and suddenly Candy feels the need to sit down. She has to find Sheriff Anderson, tell him everything, even what she saw at the jailhouse.

Patricia continues to talk. "Due to the circumstances, Sven has decided to close tonight. He wants everyone to get home safely before this maniac goes on the rampage again."

"That's awfully considerate of him. Plus, who's going to go out with a nut case on the loose?" Jimmy chimes in.

"Why don't you two close up, and then get out of here."

"What, without any perks for making the effort to get here." Jimmy whines.

"I think you've had enough, Jimmy, you were drunk when you walked in the door, and I shouldn't have given you those two right away, so no." Patricia turns toward the back office. "Just go home before I tell Sven."

Candy has never heard Patricia talk like this before. She sounds like Hector. Whipping back around to her, she softens. "Candy, I'm truly sorry for your loss, I know what you're feeling." Patricia races down the hallway, wailing as she disappears into Toth's office.

Grabbing Candy's arm, Jimmy tries to drag her to the bar. "Come on, now's our chance." He yanks a little harder. "What are ya drinkin'?"

She rips free of his grip, and steps back. "Are you nuts. Now's not the time to be doing that. Let's just get out of here, okay."

"Well, if we're not going to have it here, then I'll take something for the road." Jimmy reaches under the counter top and snags a bottle of Jack Daniels from the inventory, hurrying to stash it in his coat. Snake-eyeing Candy, he threatens. "I'll keep your little secret, if you keep mine."

He winks at her, and Candy has never felt so repulsed in her entire life. "You're turning into a drunk, you know that, right."

"It's just a phase, I have everything under control, don't you worry about me. You should be more concerned with your own well being."

Candy knows Jimmy is being a jerk because his buzz is

wearing off, and he's jonesin' for another drink. "Listen, I'm going to cruise. Do you want to drive with me and we can come back for your car tomorrow?"

"No, thank you." He snubs her. "I'm perfectly fine."

"Okay then, I'm going to hit the road, you don't mind turning the lights out and things, do you?"

"Nope, you go right ahead." Candy can tell by the look on Jimmy's face that he's heading back to the bar as soon as she leaves. "Hey, Candy." Jimmy calls out as she turns and reaches the door. "I'm really sorry about Billy. I know you're upset, even if you aren't showing it right now. If you need me later, you know where I'll be." He prances up and bear-hugs her.

"Yeah, yeah, yeah," She pushes him away. "Now get off me." Lumbering through the revolving door, Candy is whisked into a vapor lock, where for a second she feels suspended in time.

Spinning out, she gasps for air. The coldness makes her cough. Running to her car, she jumps in, and laying her head on the frigid steering wheel, Candy Jane begins to cry.

Thick, frozen tears dribble down her cheeks as heaves of agony crease her body. Uncontrollable waves rush over her like high tide. She has to get home, lock the doors, not see or talk to anyone until she can gain her composure. Jamming the gear into first, she drives away. Forceful winds rise up again, and Candy wonders if they're in for another blast from Old Man Winter.

❀ ❀ ❀

Patricia calms her shaking hands, and wipes the fake tears from her cheeks. If they were giving out awards for best performance, she would definitely win. And yes, even though she had a thing for Toth, that's all it was. Never in her life has she ever loved a man, or woman for that matter. Even her late husband was just a money cruise, there again, she should've won an award for pretending to love a man whom she never did.

Opening the office door a crack, Patricia listens to see if everyone has left. Hearing only silence, she tip-toes out to the front of the house. Thinking to herself, she needs to find Cynthia Scotchland, and finally take care of business.

7

Winds rattle the windows, making Cynthia jump in the chair. It's bad enough the room is so creepy, but having Gear's dead body right outside gives her the heebie-jeebies. She wishes the sheriff would contact her, or even that lame brain, Deputy Pickens. But she hasn't heard from either one of them, and her patience is running out.

Revenge pulsates through her veins. She knows that Candy Jane is behind these murders, and she's going to pay. But, first she has to find the wench before the sheriff arrests her, which is only a matter of time.

"Whore!" Cynthia screams. Rising, she flings the stapler against the wall, and watches as the silver staples dangle in the air, dazzling like diamonds in the late afternoon sunlight, and then dropping to the floor like bug-juiced flies.

Every raw nerve in her body pulsates, like broken live wires, spitting electricity wildly. She tries to count to ten, an exercise her therapist suggested, but it doesn't work. "Quack!" Maybe she should take care of him, too. Smiling, Cynthia rubs her chin.

Except for this unexpected delay, her plans are working out perfectly. And even doing this favor for Sheriff Anderson is proving beneficial. She's able to keep the troopers away, while giving the plows more time to clear the highway. She'll destroy the radio before she leaves, that way the sheriff can't contact anyone.

Cynthia becomes ecstatic thinking about her future. She'll take care of Candy Jane and then disappear forever. She'll get her hair done, buy a whole new wardrobe, get a total make over, start a fresh life where nobody knows her.

She'll change her name. Maybe become a distant Kennedy cousin, or something like that. The world is her oyster, Cynthia smiles, falling deeper into her fantasy. "Yup, the world is my oyster." She announces, hearing the back door creak open.

❋　❋　❋

Jimmy waits alone in the bar for a few minutes before deciding to sneak himself a drink. Patricia hasn't reappeared since Candy left, and the last of the kitchen guys have said good-bye, so basically he's on his own.

Pouring himself a hefty shot, Jimmy sits down on a stool and lights a cigarette. Taking a drag, he exhales blue smoke, and takes a sip of the Kentucky bourbon. How did he end up being the last one here, when he doesn't want to be here in the first place.

Damn, Candy Jane, and her drama. Jimmy's getting tired of the tension, and believes maybe it's time to give their friendship a little rest. He'll call her when he gets home, and talk to her about it.

"Well, I'm glad to see that you helped yourself."

Patricia's voice startles Jimmy, making him almost spill his drink. "Yeah, I figured you wouldn't mind. Everything is done, and I'm going to cruise after this, so."

"No, no, it's fine. I just have to finish up some paper work, and then I'm out of here, too." Patricia turns around.

"Hey, Patricia, I'm truly sorry about everything that happened to Toth, and all." He sounds like a recording from earlier. "Nobody deserves that, no matter how big of a jerk they are."

She faces him. "Thanks, Jimmy, that means a lot." Waving her arm toward the bar, she says. "Please, have another one, before you leave. If you'd like."

Holding his drink in the air, Jimmy responds. "Let me see how this one goes down first." Knowing perfectly well he'll take Patricia up on her offer, maybe twice. "Thanks, though."

"Good night, Jimmy."

"See ya tomorrow, Patricia." He watches as she slumps through the kitchen door, holding her bobbing head in sight until it disappears around a corner.

Jimmy listens to the restaurant silence, feeling slightly scared to be sitting alone. After all there is a serial killer on the loose, and he's targeting men. He could very well be the killers next mark. Paranoia strangles Jimmy's brain, as he downs his drink, deciding to have his next one to go.

Slipping around the bar, he makes sure Patricia is nowhere in sight before filling a paper cup with Jack Daniels, and snapping a plastic top on the rim.

Sneaking down the hallway, Jimmy stops in front of the office, and quickly announces "The front door is locked, and the lights are off, so I'm gonna cruise."

"Okay, Jimmy. See ya." Patricia doesn't lift her head from the papers she's scribbling on.

Rushing through the metal back door, he glances at the horizon. The tired yellow sun sets slowly, painting the sky a burnt orange. Skating across the iced parking lot, Jimmy slides to his car.

A calmness comes over him, as he jumps into the front seat, and twists the ignition. At first it doesn't turn over, but then on the second try, the motor revs, and jamming the stick into drive, he takes off without letting the Buick warm up.

Fishtailing out of the lot, Jimmy almost slips into a snow drift, but manages to gain control before plunging into the whiteness. Wiping his gloved hand across the fogged windshield, he whispers a silent prayer as the sun dips below the forest tree line.

❈　❈　❈

Jon Anderson taps the face of his watch, and sees the second hand tick away. It's going on five o'clock, and there's still no troopers. Unlatching the walkie-talkie from his belt, Jon presses the speak button and yells. "Cynthia, this is Sheriff Anderson, are you there?" He holds the black box up to his ear, but only hears gray static. "Cynthia, answer me, now!" He orders.

Nothing!

"Damn-it." Jon curses, suspecting she's bailed on him.

Changing the frequency, Jon speaks into the mouth piece. "Mark, this is Sheriff Anderson. Ten-four."

Jon angles the cruiser over to the side of the street, and waits for his deputy's reply. There is none. What in the hell's going on? Whatever it is, it's not good. Forgoing his plans to return to Toth's, Jon wheels around and heads toward town.

The roads are darkening as the sun disappears, and the pale blue sky fades with the light. Jon loves the intensity of the winter months. The elements are so pure and innocent, and then merciless and unforgiving. He replays Candy's reaction when he told her about Billy. Her face didn't flinch. But that really doesn't mean anything. For some people it takes a little while for things to set in before they react. The ones that have always worried Jon, were those who over-react.

Switching the lights off as he approaches the jail house, Jon pulls over slowly, and gets out of the Jeep. Drawing his weapon, he crouches along the red brick wall, sneaking to the back. He stops to peek into a window, but sees nothing.

Slithering around the corner, he's greeted with Gear's slumped over body, and suddenly feels a chill ripple through him. Caution clangs in his brain, as a shock bolt of fear jolts through him.

Slowly easing himself through the door, Jon's greeted with a still silence. Shadows ripple across the brown walls, as Sheriff Anderson tip-toes through the darkened office. His eyes begin to adjust to the dim room, as he notices the place has been trashed. Papers scattered along the floor, and the file cabinet, drawers drawn, teeters against the wall.

"What the hell?" Jon whispers silently, wondering if maybe Fruit Loops is here waiting for him. But then, what has she done with Cynthia?

Approaching the bathroom, Jon believes he hears something drop from inside. Inching closer, he places his shaking hand on the knob, and twisting the handle, flings the door open.

A stale scent greets him, accompanied by a serenade of groans. Carefully peering around the frame, Jon discovers Mark, tied and gagged, wriggling in the corner. A creek of blood trickling down his forehead.

Rushing over to him, Jon tears the gray duct tape off his mouth. Mark screams in pain.

"Damn-it, Jon, that hurts."

"I'll show you what hurts." Pushing his deputy forward, Jon slices his hands free, and then stands up. "What are you doing here?"

"Cynthia called and told me to meet you here."

"What?"

"Yeah, about an hour ago." Mark steadies himself against the wall as he rises. "So, I get here and catch her going at the radio with the fire ax. And when I go to stop her, she belts me, and here I am."

"She didn't say anything to you?"

"Nope. All I heard her say is that it's payback time for Candy Jane."

Cynthia's flipped out! He has to find her, and find her fast.

"Did she say anything else, Mark? Like where she might be heading?"

"Nope." Deputy Pickens rubs the back of his skull. "I have an awful headache, Jon."

"Take some aspirin." He's in no mood to dole out sympathy. Lumbering over to the radio, he picks up the useless crushed object. Man, she really did a number on the office, he observes.

Setting the device back down, he stomps toward the door. "Mark, you stay here. Put some ice on your cut, and just relax. I'm sure you'll be fine."

"Where you going?"

"To find Cynthia Scotchland."

Carol Anderson sits in front of Mira Mendelson's house, confused as to why she's scared. Her nerves are tingling, and she's kind of anxious, like a school girl who sees the boy she has a crush on coming toward her.

"This is ridicules." She whispers to herself, holding her breath as she scoots out of the car.

The cold is freezing, as Carol baby-steps her way onto the porch. Her shaking hand, reaches out and raps three times on the hard oak door.

Shivering, Carol waits, but hears no one approaching. This time, she rings the bell, and listens to faint chimes dangling in the back ground. But still, nothing. Maybe she's sleeping, Carol thinks, hoping she hasn't woken her.

Retreating, she suddenly hears Mira's voice.

"Carol, is that you?"

Caught off guard, she quickly turns, and wobbling, nearly falls with the cake, had it not been for Mira catching her. Both women begin to laugh hysterically, as Mira steadies Carol against the rail, their eyes catching each others in a distant memory.

Carol realizes the cold has vanished.

"I thought I'd come see how you're doing." Her breath is raspy.

Wrapping her arm around Carol's waist, Mira leads her down the steps. "Come in around back, okay. I'm still not ready to be in the front of the house yet." She tightens her hold. Carol feels like she's home.

The kitchen is warm and cozy, with the slight scent of cinnamon. Slipping out of her coat, Carol sits down at the table filled with casseroles and desserts.

"People have been stopping by all day with food. Please, help yourself."

"I wouldn't know where to begin." She smiles at Mira. "How you holding out?"

Mira shuffles over to the stove. "I guess better than I expected. I don't know, it's kind of numbing, very surreal like, I really can't describe how it feels."

"That's okay, we can talk about other things, or just sit here in silence, I don't know, whatever you'd like." Carol stands up, suddenly feeling overwhelmed, "Or, if you want to be alone, I can leave."

Mira strolls over to Carol, and the two women embrace in a longing hug.

"Carol," Mira whispers in her ear. "If there is anyone whom I'd want here, it's you."

Carol is reluctant to let go, but doesn't want to make this moment awkward. What's happening to her? It's as if a stargate of emotions is erupting, sensations of free-floating, sparking every nerve.

Releasing Mira, Carol sits back down. "I'm sorry, I don't know what's come over me." She studies Mira's face, heartbroken and aged. "I just wanted to come over and see if you needed anything, and to tell you how awful I feel about your loss."

"How about a cup of tea? I think we could both use some."

"That'd be great, Mira. But here, let me get it." Carol starts to stand, but Mira places a hand on her shoulder, stopping her from rising.

"No, I'll get it. Staying active helps me keep my mind occupied."

"Of course, I understand. I don't mind being waited on." Carol giggles, and Mira leans over and kisses her on the cheek. The soft lips tingle her sensitive skin, bringing pools of tears to Carol's eyes.

"Thank-you." Mira, turns and stands in front of the stove. "It's nice knowing how many people care. I'm surprised. This is really the first lull of the day, and hopefully, the rush is over. There are some whom I didn't even realize knew Billy. Like that Cynthia Scotchland woman. Wow, she's a strange one." Mira faces Carol. "Do you know that she actually asked me if she could see the body."

"What?"

"Honest."

"That's weird."

"She even brought a dessert. It's that carrot cake over there. I know it's store bought, but it's the thought that counts."

"Do you know her very well?"

"No, not really. I think she went to school with Billy, but I don't know how well they knew each other. I just find the whole scene rather strange."

"I understand."

Quiet enters the room, like a balloon into the sky. The two women gaze at each other. Mira sits down across from Carol and pouring two cups of tea, slides one over to her.

"Remember that time at the lake? How much fun we had, until those boys came along and started harassing us."

Before that moment, Carol had blocked the day out of her memory, but suddenly, all the sights, sounds and sensations came rushing back. It was right after that day they weren't allowed to see each other anymore. Throughout the years, Carol believed it was because of the boys, but now she recalls it might have been because of what the boys had seen.

Carol's cheeks flush. "I haven't thought of that in a long time." Smiling at Mira, she whispers. "I've never felt like that with any one since."

Mira touches the tips of Carol's fingers. "Neither have I, and I didn't realize it until I saw you again. At first I wasn't sure what I was feeling, but then that memory leaped out at me, and now it's like my heart has been jump started."

Standing, Carol's heart is weightless, as though a ton of bricks has been lifted from the lonely organ. Dizziness captures her, and she sways.

"You okay, Carol." Mira rushes to her side.

Sitting back down, Carol responds "Yes, I just got a little light headed. Thanks."

"I'm sorry Carol, I don't know what's come over me. It's like I suddenly realize how short life really is and I don't want to waste it anymore." Pulling a chair up next to Carol, Mira plops down. "Come on, you can't say you don't feel this, too."

"But Mira, your son just died, I don't believe you're thinking rationally." Mira's right though, Carol is experiencing the same feelings. But what can she do? She certainly can't act on them.

"I was more like a maid to my son than a mother. I mean, I loved him, but there were times I didn't like him." Wringing her hands. "I don't mean to sound detached, it's just that, well, it's life, and now I've been given the chance to experience another part of living, and the longer I wallow in self-pity, the further distanced I'll become from my true potential."

Mira's words echo Carol's thoughts. She's never heard her beliefs verbalized by anyone else before. It's as though they are on the same wave length. Carol doesn't mention this, though.

Feeling a little off kilter, and sensing she needs to be alone, she slides her chair back slightly, and stands, this time strong and stable on her feet. "I need to go. This is so overwhelming. Let me think about things, and maybe you should, too."

Mira rises with her. "I have, even *before* all this happened. I was just waiting for the right time to talk to you about it."

Their finger tips brush, as they face the door. Carol is electrified. Her cheeks splash with rose, as her heart flutters like a late summer butterfly.

Stroking Carol's cheek, Mira smiles. "You're a little flushed." She leans in and kisses the warm red. "Did I do that?"

Their lips are inches away from each other, and Carol inhales deeply, trying to tame her yearning tongue. She surrenders. Their mouths connect in deep seeded passion. Her mind fills with multi-colored sparklers, as she hangs tight to Mira, not wanting to let go. Their bodies magnetize each other, pulling them together with an unearthly force.

Pushing away, Carol is dazed. None of this makes sense. She swings the door open and runs down the stairs.

"Carol, wait!" Mira, pleads, reaching for her coat and dashing after her. She's too late, though. Carol is already in her car and pulling away down the slushy road.

Stunned, is all Carol can describe herself as being. What is Mira thinking? She must have really gone over the edge with Billy's death. There's no way they can be together. For one thing, she, Carol Anderson is not a lesbian. Never even had an inkling, well, maybe just one. But that was a school girl crush, and long gone by now, at least she thought it was.

Should she tell, Jon?

Her whole body is shaking. What good will it do to mention it to him. All he'll probably say is, can he watch, or maybe join in. The image repulses her. Carol is sure that after a few days, when everything settles down, Mira will see it's her delirium causing her to act this way.

But what about her? Something definitely got turned on, a switch she never knew existed. A peacefulness surrounds her now, an ease of living, so to speak. She shakes her head, trying to make sense of her thoughts.

Pulling into the garage, she sits there for a moment playing the whole scene over again in her mind. There's a familiarity in the bazaar act; it makes kissing Mira feel natural and right.

❈   ❈   ❈

Mira watches as Carol drives away into the pink hazy evening. Rubbing her head, she closes her eyes and feels a frozen tear dribble down her cheek. What did she just do? This is not what she'd planned. She was going to suggest that maybe they try to open up their friendship a little more, see what happens.

Her intent was never to maul the woman. But the moment was there, and Mira could not control herself. She remembers how Carol responded, her body softening within her arms. The heated warmth that beamed from her after they kissed.

Maybe her actions were too much, though. What if she scared Carol off, after all, the woman certainly ran away fast enough. The thought of never seeing Carol again, frightens her. It's taken a lot of courage to face up to her feelings, and then display them. The situation will be horrific if they're thrown back in her face.

Closing the door behind her, Mira shivers with the chill. As soon as the funeral is over, she'll sell the house, all of her belongings, and leave Mongoose Falls. If Carol Anderson wants to join her, that'll be wonderful. If not, she'll just have to get on with life, alone.

Candy Jane stampedes up the steps and fumbles with her keys as she tries to unlock the door. Rushing in, she closes and locks the portal. Her senses are raw. She can't think clearly. Her brain is like live wires touching and sparking, mad cobras hissing in a pit.

Flopping down on the sofa, Candy lays her head in her hands, and begins sobbing. Her whole world has come crashing down, and she doesn't know how to stop it. Now that Sheriff Anderson believes she is the killer, there's no rescue. No one will believe her. She has no alibi, and she was careless to leave that crappy cereal at every crime scene.

Can she be any dumber?

Amelia pounces up on the cushions and starts rubbing her chest against Candy's arm. She smothers the orange kitty against her breasts and snuggles her face in the furry animal while she cries. Amelia rests there content, happy to be of some comfort to her distressed friend.

Stroking the cat, Candy sobs, "Oh, Amelia, what am I going to do? I'm in big trouble, and I don't know where to turn."

Bored, the feline jumps out of her grasp, and turning to look at her, meows, and sashays away.

"Thanks, anyway. You've been a big help." The tears taper off.

Wiping her cheek dry, Candy's terrified. She's scared that the next knock, next phone call will be the sheriff wanting to arrest her. Maybe she should just turn herself in. Tell him the truth, that her involvement is just bad luck; her being in the wrong place at the wrong time.

But will he believe her?

Why not? She's doesn't have a criminal record, and she certainly doesn't display any characteristics of a serial killer. Tiny bubbles begin to pop in her head, as Candy Jane thinks she's on the verge of losing her mind. Trying to calm herself, she agrees with the voice of reason whispering to her, that it's best to surrender.

Going over to the dining room table, she grabs a pen and a piece of paper. Trying not to shake, she scratches out a note for Jimmy, giving him instructions on how to take care of Amelia while she's in the pokey. She'll leave a copy of her key under the mat, and then call him later after she's been incarcerated.

Relief spills over her, like getting rid of a bad case of hic-ups, or an unknown splinter gone infected. Smiling slightly, she sneaks over to Amelia, sleeping peacefully on the back of the couch.

Hearing the approach, the cat opens her eyes, moans in agitation of being woken up, and rolls over on her back, ex-posing a white chubby belly. Candy can see pink skin be-neath the silky fur. Bending over, she nuzzles her nose in the chalky fluff.

"Oh, you're so soft." Amelia begins to purr. Candy straightens, keeping her palm on Amelia. "I might be gone for a while, so Jimmy will look after you. I know you act as if you don't like him, but I know better. I'll keep in touch." She kisses her once more. "Bye, sweetie."

Taking one last glance around her apartment, Candy wonders if she'll ever be within these walls again. Pools be-gin to form in her eyes, as she hurriedly scampers out, hear-ing the latch lock behind her.

Breathing deeply, she holds her breath for a moment and lets the cold air burn her lungs before exhaling. "Well, all in all, it's been a good life," Candy whispers, sliding across the frozen sidewalk.

❀　❀　❀

Surprise and dismay fills Jon Anderson as he calls out to his wife, only to hear the quiet hum of the appliances. Where is she? There was a time when Carol let him know almost every move she made, but obviously, that's changing, too.

The only reason he came home is to see her, say how sorry he is for his absence, and try to explain to her, that whatever it is they're going through, they'll work it out. After all, doesn't he love Carol?

Gazing out the bedroom window, and feeling a sense of peace, Jon tries to fit the puzzle together, when a memory suddenly occurs to him. A few weeks ago he overheard Gear talking to Mark about Cynthia, and how he wishes he could dump her, but is having trouble because the sex is so good.

At the time it struck Jon odd because he thought Hector Toth and Cynthia were an item. Thinking nothing of the soap opera gossip, Jon ignored the conversation. But now, a connection is starting to form. It's not Candy Jane, but also Cynthia, who knew all three victims. But how *does* Candy Jane fit into these murders?

Feeling the vibration of the garage door opening, Jon listens as Carol's car pulls in. For a brief moment he thinks about sneaking out the front door, and dealing with this matter later. But Jon Anderson has never been a man who runs from his problems.

"Honey, you home?"

He hears Carol's voice, a sad emptiness fills him. Rubbing his face with his hands, he replies. "I'm upstairs."

❀ ❀ ❀

Still feeling light headed from Mira's kiss, Carol tries to calm her tingling body, as she calls out. "Honey, you home?"

Hearing Jon's reply, Carol's shoulders slump. All she wants to do is take a hot bath and replay the event in her mind. Her emotions agonize in unknown terror, while her heart leaps and bounds within her chest.

A change is happening. As though she's experiencing a conscious awakening. Inside she knows the life of all these years is over. Now, she has to figure out the right thing to do without anyone getting hurt.

Climbing the stairs, all Carol can think about is Mira, and how she wants to be with her. How she wishes it is her she is ascending to see, but it's not. Instead, it's Jon, and Carol expects the third degree as soon as she walks through the door. Where was she? Who was she with?

Will he be able to see her feelings etched in her blushing cheeks, or the dazzle that now reflects in her eyes? Will he notice? Holding her breath, Carol steps into their bedroom.

❀ ❀ ❀

Candy Jane parks her car behind town hall, not wanting anyone to see her. Fear pounds inside, as she's having second thoughts about turning herself in. If they find her guilty, she might never be free again.

Not really paying attention to anything else but her thoughts, Candy's about to open the door when she hears a screaming voice coming from within. Sneaking over to the back window, Candy peeks in.

"Cynthia Scotchland?" Candy whispers, wondering what she's doing here.

Every bone in Candy's body beckons her to run, but she doesn't listen and turns the cold knob. Opening the door slightly, she crawls into the shadows, and reaching the store room, ducks into the darkness.

Suddenly, a flashlight beam whips around, and Candy crotches down in a corner. The spray sails over her undetected, and then disappears. Feeling safe, she peeks through the crack and sees Cynthia rampaging the sheriff's desk, flailing papers out of the drawers as she curses.

Candy doesn't know Cynthia very well. She was a couple of years behind her in high school, and besides seeing her in Toth's office the other night, she's never associated with her, and by the looks of it, is glad she hasn't.

What a nut job!

Cynthia tornadoes through the office, turning everything not nailed down, over. "I'm going to find that tainted whore, and when I do, I'll give her what she deserves."

Cynthia's ravings increase, but suddenly stops for a moment when she discovers something in the file cabinet. "Yes!" She hisses, waving a plastic baggie marked *evidence* above her head, with what looks like a thin silver needle in it. Flailing around, Cynthia wails. "Watch out bitch, here I come!" And rushes out the front.

Waiting a few minutes to make sure she's gone, Candy trots over to the desk and notices the thin telephone directory laying open. Glancing down, she realizes the page Cynthia ripped out listed her address.

"Is that lunatic going to my house?" Candy exclaims, not hearing the footsteps pattering up from behind.

Jimmy flicks though the channels of the T.V., surfing for something to watch, but finding nothing of interest. He's antsy, but it's far too cold to be going out. So, here he is, stuck at home by himself with a stupid cat who doesn't even pay attention to him.

Reclining back in the lounger, Jimmy ponders Candy Jane's predicament. She's acting very peculiar, plus, what about her under-reaction to the murders. It's as though she has a heart of frozen steel. But then, people do react differently. Maybe he should give her a call, see how she's doing, after all, Candy Jane is the only friend he has in town, he should treat the relationship with respect.

Leaning over, he picks up the receiver, and dials her number. Popping an M&M candy into his mouth, he listens as the phone continues to ring. What is wrong with her answering machine, he questions? When she doesn't respond after nine rings, he hangs up, and wobbles to the kitchen to fetch another beer.

She probably just unplugged her phone, not wanting to talk to anyone, Jimmy deduces, as he plops back down.

Stray, surprisingly jumps up on his taunt stomach and begins kneading his abdomen. Jimmy begins to pet the feline, feeling safe and comfortable. He will try her again later.

❋   ❋   ❋

Patricia bides her time as she cruises around looking for Cynthia. She drove by her parents house earlier, and waited a little while for any sign of her, and when there was none, she went on the hunt.

Spying Candy's car at the sheriff's office, Patricia eases around a corner, and parks at a focal point on the street. Leaving the engine running for warmth, she waits patiently for Candy to come out. Even better though, it's Cynthia who barges out of the front door, and scampers to the back.

"What is the trollop doing?" She asks herself in a whisper. Whatever it is, it can't be good, Patricia shakes her head as she wipes the misting windows clean.

8

Candy Jane awakes, head throbbing, hands tied behind her back, choking on the handkerchief stuffed in her mouth.

"My, my, my, look who I found." Cynthia sneers at Candy, as she towers over her, then without warning, kicks her in the gut.

The pain is immense, as Candy scrunches her knees up to her chin.

Cynthia begins to circle her like a vulture over a corpse. "You know, I was just about to head over to your house, and have a little talk with you, but here you are, saving me a trip out in the cold. That's very thoughtful." She spits on Candy. "I'm sure you must be comfortable, laying there on the floor. I know you're used to it, being on your back for all those men."

Rolling the desk chair upright, Cynthia sits down and leans over, hissing. "I just want to know why you killed them. I can see why you murdered Billy. You probably found out we made love, and then maybe you got rid of Toth and Gear because you knew how much they loved me. All in the name of jealousy, is that it Candy Jane?"

Cynthia stands, flinging the chair back against the wall with her calves. "Now, though, you're going to write your confession. Admitting to all three murders, and then when they find you at the bottom of the ravine, all broken and tattered, the sheriff's mystery will be solved."

Realizing Cynthia has gone off the deep end, and that her predicament is grave, Candy tries to think of something she can do to free herself.

Slapping a pen and paper in front of Candy, Cynthia continues ranting. "Plus, you're such a dumb-ass, scattering cereal around at the crime scenes, that crap you've been devouring for who knows how long. I mean, how stupid can you be? Fruit Loops the Serial Killer, what a hoot. A part of me wants to confess to the murders, just so people will call me that. I'd be infamous."

"This girl is nuts." Candy thinks, beginning to have trouble breathing through her blood encrusted nostrils. Moaning, Cynthia looks at her, and trying her best to indicate that she can't breathe, the mad woman comes over and rips the taped gag out of Candy's mouth.

The sudden rush of air makes her cough, and she leans over, her lungs burning with each inflation. Candy gasps. "I didn't kill anybody. I don't know what you're talking about."

Cynthia towers over Candy, raging fists flailing in the air.

"Don't lie to me, I know all about you, and your devious schemes."

"Cynthia, you've been misinformed. Now, untie me, and we can discuss this like two adults. Okay?" Candy's sweating.

"No, it's not, *okay*! You had sex with Toth, an unforgivable act." She drops to the floor and glares at Candy in the eyes. "And for that, you'll die." She reaches down to untie Candy's ankles. Looking up, she threatens. "Don't try anything funny."

Just as Cynthia's warning her, Candy Jane slams her foot into her captures crotch. The woman bends over, crippled by the blow.

Standing on numb legs, Candy wobbles to the door, her tightly tied wrist bleeding red. Stumbling out onto the low porch she falls, landing in the freezing snow. Struggling to get up, Candy glances behind, trying to see if Cynthia is following her, but there is no sign. "Guess I kicked her bells off." Candy chuckles to herself.

Diving into the hatchback, she starts the vehicle. Scooting down the road, she turns at the first side street, and pulls over to the snow piled curb.

Leaning across the seat, she punches the button of the glove compartment, and as it springs open, loose papers and envelopes come spilling out. Making a feeble attempt to catch them, Candy searches for the red Swiss Army knife tucked deep in back. Thankful she recalled it was hidden there.

Slicing the ropes to freedom, Candy rubs the sore skin,

and stuffs the blade into her pocket. She doesn't have time for lolly-gagging, and needs to get help. She has to find the sheriff, otherwise, her demise is inevitable. Goose bumps cover her bone white skin, as she shakes her ghostly hands.

With the head lights off, Candy Jane Cane eases her car down the slick street. Pulling in front of Billy's house, Candy has no idea how she got here, it's as though she blacked out and this is where her auto pilot landed.

Parking on the side, Candy stares at the dark house. The only light on is in Mrs. Mendelson's upstairs bedroom. Candy wonders about the sorrow she must be feeling tonight.

Cynthia Scotchland scoops some snow into a plastic bag and returns to the sheriff's desk. She lays the compress in her lap, moaning at the coldness. "I'm gonna kill that skank." She curses, raging anger washing away any common sense.

What she needs to do is find the tease, and exterminate the vermin from the face of the earth once and for all. First though, she has to write Candy's letter, confessing to all three murders, and her own. Scribbling down the words, Cynthia designs Candy's suicide.

Smiling, with an idea in place, she stands up, and throws the ice pack against the far wall. The baggie shatters upon impact, exploding crystals everywhere. Cynthia howls out loud like a rabid coyote. Rushing to the storage closet, she flips on the light, and finds what she needs immediately.

Hanging the coil of rope around her shoulder, Cynthia plans to cruise by Candy's house first, just in case she really is that stupid, and goes home. Then she'll drive by that fairies house.

Rushing out the back door, Cynthia is startled as it bangs shut, whipping the confession off the desk. The yellow sheet slides under the file cabinet like a deflated ghost. In her hurry, Cynthia doesn't notice the gold earring laying in the corner, or hear the canting breaths billowing from the bathroom. She doesn't see the steel blue eyes slicing right through her as she trots by.

Cynthia is oblivious to the fact that now, she too, is prey.

They stand looking at each other, the silence becoming unbearable. Carol breaks the quiet. "I wasn't expecting you back so soon. Did you solve the case?" She moves over to the vanity and takes off her watch.

"No, not yet, it's becoming more complicated."

"I'm sorry to hear that." She can't face him.

"We'll get to the bottom of it." Pausing for a moment, Jon continues. "So, where've you been?"

Carol's heart leaps, and she doesn't know why, it's not as though she's done anything wrong. "I went over to see Mira, try to comfort her a little."

"And did it help?" Jon feels relief.

Carol thinks of the kiss. "Yes, I believe it did."

"Well, that's good." Jon strolls to the bed and sits down.

Leaning over, he places his head in his hands, like a man about to receive the death sentence. "Carol, are you seeing someone?"

"What? What are you talking about?"

"Are you having an affair with another man?"

"My gosh, Jon, no!" She's not lying. "Why would you think that?"

He stands. "I don't know, it just seems like lately we haven't been getting along very well, and you know, the bed has been a little cold, and I was just wondering if maybe somebody else has peaked your interest."

She saunters over to him, and holds his hand resting at his sides. Rising on her toes, she kisses his cheek tenderly. "Jon, Anderson, you know you're the only man for me."

Still not lying.

"Then, what's going on?"

"I don't know, Jon. I just haven't been feeling very sexual, that's all. Maybe it's a phase I'm going through, but it doesn't mean that I'm going to run off and find another man. I would think you'd know me better by now."

"I do know you, that's why I'm worried. You just seem so pre-occupied lately, and your attention certainly hasn't been on me at all. So, of course, I'm beginning to wonder."

Carol returns to the vanity and sits down in her chair. "Is that why you're home? Because you thought you might catch me in the throes of my lover?"

"No, no, no." He moves closer to her, and squatting, places his hand on her thigh, she flinches at his touch. Standing abruptly, Jon's anger flares. "See, that's what I mean. It's as though you think I have a fungus or something. Even the slightest stroke makes you cringe."

Carol tries to calm him down, sensing he's about ready to explode. "Jon, please, don't be ridicules. I love your touch, but I'm trying to explain to you that right now I just don't enjoy it as much. Can't you understand that, I'm sorry, but there's really nothing I can do. I'm not going to force myself to have sex with you when I don't feel like it. Is that what you want?"

"No, of course not, I just want you to tell me what happened?"

"I don't know, Jon. That's just it."

Leaning over, he tries to kiss her, but Carol evades his attempt. This time the anger barges through, and he reels on her. "Fine then, maybe I'll just go find it somewhere else."

Storming out of the room, she hears him slam the door downstairs. Carol doesn't know what's gotten into her husband, but what she does know, is that she doesn't feel the same about him.

❄ ❄ ❄

Candy Jane Cane sits in front of Billy's house. Wiping the tears from her face, she realizes deep down, she really did love Billy. Her aching heart tells her this.

Deciding it isn't doing her any good drowning in her own sorrows, she puts the car into gear, and slowly drives away. Jimmy's her best option. She can hide out there until they contact Sheriff Anderson. Candy's positive Cynthia doesn't know where Jimmy lives, so she'll be safe.

"Geeze." Candy whispers out loud, still unable to believe how crazy Cynthia has become. She's totally snapped, and Candy is realizing how dangerous the woman really is.

Has it only been twenty-four hours ago since she found Billy's body?

Creeping along the one lane street, and not really paying attention to anything but her thoughts, Candy Jane is startled when she spots a pair of head lights approaching her at high speed. Suddenly, goose-bumped dread coats her skin, as a cold clamminess brings shivers.

Cynthia!

Panic ripples along her spine, as she looks for a place to turn in, and just at the moment of impact, she punches the accelerator, and whipping right, pulls into the high school parking lot. She can hear metal scratching against the frozen snow banks.

Glancing behind her, she's amazed as the Jeep blitzes by, Cynthia's frozen face pressed to the windshield. She needs to high-tail it, before the lunatic turns around.

Putting her foot on the gas, the car lurches forward and stalls. "Shit!" Candy hisses,

forcefully turning the key in the ignition. As the engine sputters to life, Candy senses Cynthia is waiting for her at the exit driveway. She'll have to go back up the way she came. The spikes that puncture your tires when you go the wrong way should be well covered by the snow, a fact Cynthia didn't think of.

Candy Jane prays she's right, and is not about to drive

into her claws. Headlights off, she turns around, and creeps down the driveway, holding her breath as she turns onto the street. By now, Cynthia will have guessed that she's not coming out the exit, and will be racing back here instead.

❀   ❀   ❀

Cynthia Scotchland pounds the steering wheel, while screaming at the top of her lungs. "I'll get you, bitch. You just wait." She slaps the dash board hysterically.

Drool dribbles down her chin, she quickly swipes it away with her sleeve. That's it, Cynthia isn't going to let Candy slip away again. If she was focused more, none of this cat and mouse chase would be happening.

But that's okay, Cynthia reassures herself, she's got Candy exactly where she wants her, now.

Realizing it's taking Candy Jane a long time to drive through the parking lot, it occurs to Cynthia that she must've turned around, and gone back the way she came. And now she's gotten away again.

Shaking her head, and becoming more furious by the minute, Cynthia peels away, and speeds to the front, where she sees no sign of Candy or her car. "Damn-it." She squeals, slamming her hand against her forehead.

"I can't believe you let her get away. You idiot."

Cynthia hears a voice, and glances around, but there's no one else in the jeep. Her left eye begins to twitch, and she rubs the jumping nerve until the socket tears up.

"You need to go find her." Her ghost whispers.

She rather welcomes the unknown speaker, and feels comfort in hearing his cadence.

"Now!" He taunts.

Cynthia has no idea where she's going; all she knows is, at last, she has a cohort. Believing Candy Jane is on her way to gay Jimmy's house, Cynthia and her new buddy rally into the darkening evening. But first they need to make a pit stop, see if the sheriff received his love letter from Candy.

The duo howls in laughter, as Cynthia detours back downtown.

Jon Anderson can't contain his anger any longer, as he stops the snow mobile in the middle of Old Man Cruthers field. Tearing off his hat, and throwing it in the air, he jumps up and begins stomping his feet in the crunchy snow.

"Fuck, fuck, fuck!" He screams, as he kicks ice chunks with his steel toed boots.

Twirling, he slips and falls to his knees. A roar of laughter escapes Jon as he sits down on the frozen ground. What is happening? It's as though his whole world is falling apart. He's inept at his job; look at the mess the investigation is in. And his marriage; by the sounds of it, Carol is ready to pack her bags and get the hell out of Dodge.

What has he done to deserve all of this?

Rubbing snow on his face, Jon stands up, figuring sitting and sulking isn't doing him any good while a crazed serial killer runs rapid. Plus, he's getting cold. Creeping along in the dismal night, Jon gets lost in the beauty of the dusk sky, when he notices an orange glow in the distance, coming from the direction of town. It's a peculiar color, as the light dances in the black sky. Realizing what it must be, he accelerates, zipping through the graying white.

❊   ❊   ❊

A soft light shadows the dim office as Cynthia sneaks back in. Her new friend has convinced her to torch the jailhouse, destroying any evidence that might point to her, and the first thing is the letter. It has her finger prints all over it.

Cynthia is thankful for the arrival of her new mate, just in time, too. Her ideas are proving fruitless, but now, everything is new and stimulating, as if he's breathing fresh life into her. Whomever he may be. Smiling to herself, she searches the messy desk for the slip of paper, but doesn't see it. Has the sheriff already been here and retrieved it?

Madness arises in Cynthia's spine, as she douses the area with kerosene.

"Hurry up, do it, we're running out of time." Tony whispers in her ear.

"Shut up!" She's starting to get tired of his nagging. "I'm running the show here, you're just along for the ride." The empty room echoes her words. "So zip it."

Sprinkling a path of fluid to the door, she sets a book of matches at the end, and ignites the pack with her lighter. The sulfur puffs to life, spilling into flammable liquid. Cynthia watches the fiery trail reach the saturated desk top and explode. The flames rush at her, stepping back, she's barely missed by the blaze.

The beauty mesmerizes her, as the rosy glow follows Cynthia out of the burning building in search of her prey. This time, she promises, there'll be no escape.

❋ ❋ ❋

His thoughts run wild. Is Cynthia crazy enough to burn down town hall?

It doesn't take him long to get to Main Street, and as he turns onto the now crowded road, Jon sees the fire trucks parked in front of the jail.

Dashing up to the chief, Jon reaches for his arm and twirls him around.

"Jasper, what's going on here?"

The aging, rotund man turns toward Sheriff Anderson. "Damn-it, Jon, where've you been? No one could get hold of you?"

"I'm working a case. What happened?"

"We suspect arson. We got lucky though, and saved the structure. We lost almost everything inside, though. You know, the furniture and stuff." The fire marshal looks around, and then leans in close to Jon. "We found the body out back. Is there something you need to tell me?"

"It's part of the investigation, which I can't talk about, yet, Jasper. You understand, right. I had to keep the deceased outside until the medical examiner can pick the corpse up."

"Who is it, Jon?"

"I can't tell you that, either." Jon pats his long time friend's shoulder. "Sorry, protocol."

Moving closer to the still smoking building, Jon asks. "Is it okay if I go in?"

"I suppose, Jon. There are still a few hot spots that you want to watch out for, but other than that, it should be fine." He heads toward the door. "Hey, Jon, wait." The sheriff glances back, and sees Jasper handing him a flashlight. "Here, you might need this."

"Thanks." Entering the charred room, Jon shines the light across the blackened walls, noticing that his desk is now supported by four burnt peg legs, reminding him of a battered pirate. All his papers are ash, and the picture of Carol that he keeps on his desk, now, just a glob of melted goo.

Scanning the far wall, Jon trounces over to the file cabinet, still intact and stares at it. Noticing white underneath, he shifts the drawers slightly, and retrieves the piece of paper only singed at the corner. He quickly bends over and picks it up. Shining the torch closer to the letter, Jon begins to read the scribbled words:

Dear Sheriff Anderson,

First and foremost I want to apologize for all the trouble that I have been causing lately. I don't know what has gotten into me, but it has ruined my life and those whom I killed. Therefore, I've decided to end my existence on this earth before I hurt anyone else. I'm sorry for lying to you.

Yours Truly,
Fruit Loops the Serial Killer
(AKA) Candy Jane Cane

Jon knows halfway through the scribbled suicide/confession note that Candy Jane did not write this letter, but Cynthia Scotchland did, which only means that the real Fruit Loops has captured Candy Jane, and is about to kill again.

Yanking open the charred top drawer, Jon scrambles the contents, but sees no plastic baggie. She must've stolen the stiletto, too, Jon frets, slamming the cabinet shut. He needs to take action, and take it fast.

❄ ❄ ❄

Jimmy believes he hears a car outside, and hopes it's Candy. He peeks through the curtain again, but the neighborhood is empty, except for what looks like an abandoned vehicle parked across the street.

Muffled sirens ruffle his feathers, as goose-bumps appear on his arms. He hopes Candy is all right. He should've been there more when she needed his help. Instead, he'd been the same old kind of jerk he always is, putting himself first, before anyone else.

He senses Candy is in some kind of trouble, and maybe, just maybe he subconsciously doesn't want to get involved.

What kind of ally is that?

Releasing the lace drape, Jimmy turns around and screeches when he sees Cynthia Scotchland standing there. "What are you doing here?" He scampers behind a chair. "How did you get it?"

She steps closer to him. "I'll ask the questions, fag."

"Hey, that's not very nice."

"Shut up!" She screams, raising shivers across Jimmy's skin. He knows this is not a social call. "Where's Candy Jane?"

"Candy Jane?" He believed Cynthia was here to rob him. Some where he'd heard, she used to B&E all the time. It could've been a rumor though, as he watches her produce a silver, thin knife.

"What's that?"

"Your destiny, if you don't tell me where that whore is."

Jimmy continues to back up. He can see the insanity blaze in her eyes as she approaches him.

"Now, listen Cynthia, there's no reason to go off the deep end, here. Maybe we should just sit down, have a beer and relax, doesn't that sound better. You can tell me what's wrong, and maybe I can help."

"Ha! You help. You couldn't pull your ass out of a hole in the ground."

Jimmy feels a blasting shock, like battery wires being connected to his brain, as he realizes he's face to face with Fruit Loops the Serial Killer.

"You're him, I mean her, aren't you?"

"What are you talking about?" Cynthia continues her rampage through the house.

"You're Fruit Loops the Serial Killer?"

Cynthia's heart swells with pride, as Tony whispers congratulations in her ear. "Yes, I am. But you won't be around long enough to spread the news." Cynthia rushes at him. "Now, where is she?"

Jimmy is surprised when she grabs the back of his shirt and yanks him toward her. It's as if she has super natural powers that are defenseless. She tosses him on the floor.

"I'm telling you, I don't know where she is. The last time I saw her was when she left work, and that was a few hours ago." Jimmy cowers away in fear. This woman *is* a lunatic.

Towering over him, Cynthia lifts Jimmy up and leading him to a chair, forces him to sit down. Stray appears, and begins rubbing up against Jimmy's leg, begging for food.

"This is not the time, Stray. Quick, run and get help." The orphan plops down and starts licking herself. Jimmy wishes Candy Jane would have found a dog.

Bending down, Cynthia picks up the cat and throws her against the wall. Stray, bounces off it and falls to the floor on all fours, scampering away to safety.

"Hey, don't do that. She has nothing to do with this." Now, Jimmy's getting mad.

Making an attempt to stand up, Cynthia pushes him back down by the shoulders, and leans in close to his face.

"You listen to me, and listen to me good. I don't want to kill you, I have no qualms with you. But if you push me any further I will, do you get my drift."

Turning his head to the side, Jimmy spits. "You need a breath mint."

The sting across his cheek from Cynthia's slap is red hot. She might have loosened a couple of teeth. He feels a tiny stream of blood ease down his chin, and wipes it away with the back of his hand.

"Now, are you going to take me seriously?"

Shocked and scared, Jimmy doesn't respond as Cynthia twirls a roll of duct tape around her wrist. Ripping a length of gray adhesive off, she lines it up on Jimmy's mouth, and pats the gag tight.

"Don't forget to do his arms and legs." Tony instructs.

"Shut up, I'm not stupid." Cynthia yells out, as Jimmy, wide-eyed, cringes back.

Tying his legs together, she then bounds his arms behind his back. The stinging burn of the staggering circulation fills his veins, and Jimmy believes that if someone doesn't come to his rescue quickly, he might die.

Scampering around the room, while wringing her hands together, Cynthia stops in front of him, her face, red and pulsing. "Now, you listen to me, one of the reasons why I'm keeping you alive is so that you can tell everyone the truth about these murders. You tell them that Fruit Loops the Serial Killer is Cynthia Scotchland, *not* Candy Jane Cane. That glory should be mine, not that whore's." She waves her finger in front of Jimmy's face. "You got that? You tell everyone the truth after they find Candy's body dangling from Maynard's Bridge." Running out the door, she leaves the portal ajar.

She's going to kill Candy.

"Oh, my, gosh," Jimmy's mind screams. He needs to get free and find help. Is this really happening? He feels sick to his stomach, but knows if he throws up he'll choke. The cold air whips in from the open gateway, cooling him off, helping him to control the nausea.

Trying to wriggle his hands free, Jimmy realizes the tape is to snug. He hears a scratching at the back of the chair, and careens around to see Stray tearing at the tape. There must be a scent she's smelling, or is she that smart, Jimmy thinks as gray shreds began to flitter to the floor.

9

Carol Anderson is beside herself. Tears well up in her eyes, as chaos roams her brain. What is she thinking, believing that she and Mira can build something together, the idea's absurd.

But her heart disagrees.

Laying down on the bed, a gush of remorse swells over her. This fall-out isn't her fault. If Jon hadn't been so pushy and demanding lately, she might want to think about reconciling with him. The feelings have changed though, at least hers did, even before this incident with Mira.

Glancing around the room she's slept in for the past two decades, Carol tries to recall a time when she's felt the same sensations with Jon, as she does with Mira, but can't. There is nothing to compare it to. That in itself has to tell her something.

Life pours out of her, streaming like trout filled creeks, giving her hope, purpose. But at the same time, the idea of hurting Jon makes Carol reconsider her intentions. Her heart sinks at the thought. A black shriveled pit, in an empty vessel of a woman.

She has to decide!

Her body tingles with daydreams of Mira: spring is in the air. She smells the sweet, mouth-watering scent of lilacs. Bolting upright, she rubs her hands through her hair, and rushes to retrieve her coat. A driving force catapults Carol into her car, as she speeds and spins to the Mendelson's house. The thought of being away from Mira for a minute more, is driving Carol crazy.

❄ ❄ ❄

Candy Jane hides in the shadows, peering around the corner of the house, watching as Cynthia leaves Jimmy's. If Candy had not dropped her keys outside the door, she wouldn't have heard Cynthia's voice, and instead would've barged right into her demise. Running for cover, she ducks behind a snow crusted bush just in time before Cynthia turns to look. In her haste, Cynthia loses her balance, and slips on the ice, falling hard on the frigid ground.

Candy can't control a giggle. Hearing the chuckle, Cynthia looks in her direction, and catching a glimpse of Candy's orange coat, scrambles to her feet, and runs after her. Fearing for her life, Candy tries to jet away, but the traction is bad and her boots slip on the first try.

Finally able to get her feet beneath her, Candy hides behind the aluminum shed, searching for any sign of Cynthia, but there is none. No crunching snow, or heavy breaths, just the silence of the winter night.

Believing she's safe, Candy runs up the back stairs, and before reaching the top, feels a blow to her head. Her body collapses, as she falls into the snow like a lifeless puppet. Laying still, Candy listens to the twinkling stars singing above her. A shaded face leans over hers, blocking the moon from sight, kind of like an eclipse, Candy thinks, as her world goes black.

Patricia slouches down in her seat as she watches Cynthia abduct Candy Jane. The windows have long frosted over, and the little hole to peek out of is starting to coat with ice. She'll follow Cynthia to where ever she's going, and after she frees Candy Jane, she'll take care of her nemesis.

Patricia isn't sure if she's more mad at Cynthia for sleeping with Toth, or that she's taking credit for the murders. After sneaking up to the house and hearing her brag about how she's the real Fruit Loops the Serial Killer, Patricia felt a rage she's never felt before course through her chilled veins. Now, they'll be no mercy.

Starting the car as Cynthia takes off in Jimmy's junker, Patricia eases out of the darken parking spot, not turning on her lights, as she crawls behind her next victim.

❀   ❀   ❀

Her house is dark and silent, with fresh footprints every-where.

"Damn-it," Sheriff Anderson hisses, trudging around to the back, and noticing the kitchen window is broken. He figures Cynthia must be on the hunt.

Drawing his gun as he opens the door and steps in, a sense a familiarity washes over him, as he slinks through the house. He's never been here before, but it feels like home.

Turning on a light as he passes by an end table, Jon notices that the place has been destroyed, with most of the drawers pulled out and the furniture over-turned. Reaching the conclusion that there's no one else in the house, Jon holsters his revolver, and enters Candy's bedroom. Sensations of infidelity ripple through him, and he doesn't know why. It's not as though he's doing anything weird.

Amelia meows as Jon shuffles by the bed. Bending over, he pets the feline, who obviously is unaffected by the disaster surrounding her. Where could Candy be? Jon asks himself, coming up with the answer quickly.

"Jimmy's!" He sputters out loud, racing to the snow mobile. That's the only other place Jon knows Candy will feel safe. Timber-wolves howl in the crystal black night, sending shivers down Jon's spine.

❀   ❀   ❀

Candy Jane awakes groggy and confused. Everything is dark, and the first thing she smells is exhaust. She must be in a trunk of a car, she deduces; Cynthia has caught her. Panic rips across her brain as she rolls back and forth, knocking her head against the metal frame. She feels like a dolphin caught in a tuna can.

Throbbing pain comes from the lump on her head, as she recalls being at Jimmy's, and now, captured. Candy doesn't know what she's going to do. Her hands and legs are taped, and the sticky adhesive layer on her mouth is rough and dirty.

Candy prays this lunatic hasn't harmed Jimmy, or Stray for that matter. She wouldn't be able to live with that, even though her life *is* heading toward an early end. A sense of guilt sinks in, as she thinks about the men who died, or got hurt because of her. Maybe she doesn't deserve to live, and Cynthia is her saving grace.

Her body bruises from the beating of the bumpy ride. Sensing that the car is slowing down, Candy tries to think fast of a plan to escape. But how? She can barley move, and her muscles feel all tight and cramped. Without warning, the trunk flies open, and a blast of cold air stings her face.

"Get out, bitch!" Cynthia hoists Candy Jane from the steel box, and pushes her onto a sled.

Candy Jane rolls off the wooden boards, figuring it might help delay the inevitable. Maybe give whomever might be looking for her, a little more time, *if,* anyone is searching for her.

Anger rages through Cynthia as she drops down in the

snow, and holds a pistol to Candy's temple. Now, she's really scared. "You wanna mess with me, whore? I'll blast you to smithereens right here and now, without a second thought. Is that what you want?" Cynthia stands and kicks Candy in the back. The blow streaks through her kidneys, searing jolts soar through her.

Amazed at Cynthia's strength, Candy lays motionless as the petit woman rolls her back onto the Jet Flyer. "Now, stay!"

Doom lingers over the trembling woman, like a black cloud on a wedding day, as Candy begins to convince herself that she'll never be saved, and that these are the last precious moments of her time on earth. It makes her sad to think that she will never see Amelia or Jimmy again. Never tell her mom how sorry she truly is for the way their relationship has turned out.

If by some miracle Candy survives this craziness, she'll make amends to all those she has hurt; maybe do some community work. Something to change her karma, because obviously, it's bankrupt.

Gazing up, she sees the thumbnail moon hanging in the blistering black sky. A tear rolls out of her eye as she is mesmerized by the beauty surrounding her. Sparkling pin-needled Evergreens still coated in frozen white, glistening off of each other. It's like a fairyland. The woods smothered quiet, except for Cynthia's erratic panting.

Peace swims through Candy Jane as she inhales deeply, and awaits her destiny.

Neither women noticing the trail of Fruit Loops falling

out of her pocket.

❋　❋　❋

Deciding to stop at Cynthia's house before going over to Jimmy's, Sheriff Anderson is met by her mother and stepfather, who aren't the most cooperative, as he has trouble convincing them to let him in without a warrant. Finally they consent, and allow Jon in, though reluctantly.

Switching the light on in Cynthia's bedroom, Jon gags as he inhales the stale air, and old perfume scents. The area is a mess with clothes thrown everywhere, and grease stained pizza boxes covering the floor and dresser. Crushed coke cans are scattered on top of the rubble.

"Man!" Hesitantly, and a little afraid something might run out at him, Jon starts to search through the pile, hoping to find a clue as to where Cynthia might be. He opens the closet door and is caught off guard by the collage pinned to the wall.

Random pictures of Candy Jane, all meshed together.

Recent photos of Candy at work and in her home. Some show her going into Billy's house, and another one as she talks to Toth. This case goes a lot deeper than Jon imagined. He now believes Cynthia committed the murders out of jealousy, but there seems to be a darker resentment to this plot.

Dashing out of the house without stopping to thank the Scotchlands, Jon jumps into the Blazer and skids away. He has to get to Jimmy's, and fast. Heavy snowflakes masks his windshield as he tries to race through town, but is inhibited once again by the worsening weather.

❋   ❋   ❋

Carol Anderson finds herself sitting in front of Mira Mendelson's house, scared to go ring the door bell. An action that might change her existence forever, and she's not sure she's ready for that. After all, Carol is on the brink of destroying the only life she knows.

White fluffy crystals begin to descend upon the car, reminding Carol of Christmas. Pangs of sadness stream in her as memories of warm, cozy holidays ramble through her mind.

Is this the right thing?

Her heart says, yes, but her reasoning keeps her hesitant. What if things don't work out with Mira? If after a while, when the thrill wears off, and they both begin to see that maybe they made a mistake. Then where will she be?

Just as she's about to turn the car back on, Carol notices that Mira is standing at the front door. Seeming to sense Carol's doubts, the coatless woman steps forward, and waves.

As though drawn by a force greater than herself, Carol unlatches the door and crawls into the frigid air. She's not cold at all. All of the elements of tension are forgotten the moment she sees Mira.

Mounting the porch, she falls into Mira's arms, tears instantly pour from her rescued heart. Melting into the security of her embrace, Carol has never felt such a comforting warmth.

Leading her inside, Mira closes the door, and lifts Carol's face to hers, kissing her gently. "Hi!" She soothes.

"Hi!" Carol coos, resting her head on Mira's shoulder.

"I wasn't sure if I'd see you again." Mira's voice quivers.

"I'm scared."

"Me, too."

Holding hands, they float back to the kitchen, and directing Carol to sit down, Mira strolls over to the stove and retrieves a teapot. Pouring the Chai into two mugs, she sits down and lays her hands on Carol's.

"We don't have to rush. The most important thing is that we found each other and are willing to be open about our feelings, right?"

"Yes." Taking a sip of tea, Carol continues. "I just don't understand how this happened. I mean, it never crossed my mind, but then suddenly, I can't think of anything but us, or keep my hands off you."

Both women giggle, and Mira reaching up, strokes the side of Carol's face.

"You're so beautiful, you always have been."

"No, I'm not, you're just saying that."

"I'm serious." Standing, Mira holds Carol's hands easing her up. "Let's go to my room, it's a little more comfortable."

Showing no reluctance, she follows Mira up the back landing and into the sweet jasmine scent of her bedroom. Leaving the door ajar, Mira begins kissing Carol deeply on the mouth.

A gravity-free lightness washes over her, as Carol's whole

body gushes. They stumble back to the bed, playfully falling onto the firm mattress.

❅ ❅ ❅

The excitement for Jimmy Prescott when Stray first began scratching at the duct tape is long gone. Now he's, scared and distressed, and losing sensation in his limbs. His future looks dismal, plus, his bladder is so full, he thinks it might burst at any moment.

How embarrassing will that be when someone comes to rescue him. Here he'll sit, cheeks chapping in urine soaked pants. Trying not to think of his predicament, he wiggles his hands behind him, hoping to loosen the slightly frayed bondage.

Poor, Candy Jane, Jimmy sympathizes. He's frightened for her. He witnessed Cynthia clubbing her over the head, and then dragging her away. There's no way he could've warned her, the gag over his mouth muffled his cries.

He has to get free, go help Candy Jane. Closing his eyes, Jimmy tries to recall where Cynthia said she's taking her. Thinking he hears something outside, Jimmy frantically listens for another sound, but hears none. His brief hope, shot down.

"Maynard's Bridge!" Came a distant screaming voice inside Jimmy's head. That's it! That's where Cynthia is going to hang Candy.

A narrow streak of light pierces Jimmy's eyes, making him squint. As it comes closer, Jimmy suspects it's a car, and prays Cynthia hasn't returned to finish him off. But all of a sudden, just like on the silver screen, Sheriff Anderson burst through the door with his gun drawn.

Seeing Jimmy, he holds his finger to his lips, and silently takes a quick tour around the house. Returning, he rips the tape off Jimmy's mouth, and then begins slicing the bonds around his wrists and ankles.

Hacking from the gush of air, Jimmy spits out. "Sheriff, Sheriff, we need to go to Maynard's Bridge. That's where Cynthia plans on killing Candy Jane. We have to hurry."

"Calm down, Jimmy, don't go getting worked up."

"But Sheriff, it's Cynthia Scotchland who's the real Fruit Loops the Serial Killer."

"Yes, Jimmy I know."

Trying to stand, Jimmy plops back down in the chair, his legs having fallen to sleep during their inactivity. "Just give me a second, Sheriff, and I'll be ready to go."

"I can't take you with me." Jon checks his revolver, making sure it's fully loaded. "I'd get in big trouble if you got hurt."

"I'll stay out of the way. You just might need me, and I won't be there, and then you'll regret it."

He's right. Jon has no idea where his only deputy is, and doesn't have the time to find out. A second pair of eyes will be a good thing, he concludes, turning toward the door. "Well, let's go."

"Hold on." Jimmy says, tripping to the bathroom. "Just one quick pit stop."

"Hurry, up. Every second is valuable." Jon surveys the

messy room. "And put something warm on, we're going to stop and get the snow mobile, it'll be faster." Jon orders.

Reappearing, Jimmy throws his coat on, and tugs a ski-mask over his head. "Okay, let's ride."

❀ ❀ ❀

"Damn-sonovabitch." Cynthia screams, kicking the stuck tire. She should have been a little more careful coming around that bend, now the car is embedded in the embankment, and she'll have to pull Candy on a sled the rest of the way.

Scurrying to the rear of the car, she inserts the key into the frozen lock, and at first it doesn't turn, but with a second try, she hears the clank of the latch unlocking, and stands back as the trunk springs open.

Yanking Candy's numb body out of the compartment, she tosses her onto the sled, and losing her grip, watches as she rolls off the wooden frame. Fuming, Cynthia goes over, and kicks her, flipping her enemy back onto the icy planks.

"Stay on this time, or I'll use your back as the sled."

Surprisingly, Cynthia rips the tape off of Candy's mouth. A searing red pain ignites throughout her face, and at that moment, Candy swears off wax and peel jobs.

"Gosh, Cynthia…"

She belts Candy before she finishes the sentence. "Shut up." She rages over her, as warm blood drips from her nose. "You'll talk when I give you permission." The crazed woman prances around. "One more word and I'll put this back on." She dangles the filthy tape in front of Candy's face.

Grabbing the rope, she pulls the sled behind her. Candy can hear her huffing and puffing, and realizes that if she keeps up at this slow pace, help will surely get here in time.

But then again, nobody knows where she is.

Stopping suddenly, Cynthia turns toward Candy Jane, and whips out a hunting knife from the sheath at her side. Candy believes for sure this is the end. Cynthia's going to slit her throat, right here and now. All of her blood will ooze into the virgin white snow. What a horrific scene that will be. Candy giggles to herself, as she's starting to feel a little light headed.

"Get up, slut." Feeling the tape tear from around her ankles, Candy stiffens as Cynthia yanks the rope, tugging her off the flyer. "You're too big of a fat ass for me to pull you; we'll have to walk." She pushes Candy in front of her. "And don't try any funny business. Got it?" Cynthia angles the tip of the knife underneath Candy's ear lobe.

For a brief instant, Candy wants to run, but with Cynthia's arsenal, she probably won't get far. She'll be half way down the path and be lassoed by *Fruit Loops the Serial Killer*.

Why did she need rope, anyway?"

All at once, Candy figures out Cynthia's plan. She's going to hang her from Maynard's Bridge. The Angel of Death hovers above her, as Candy's shoulders suddenly become heavy. Wavering, she almost faints, but Cynthia loops her arm in Candy's and steadies her. "Oh, no you don't. No passing out on me." She tosses snow in her face, as Candy

Jane twists her head away from the ice.

"You know, Candy Jane. You wouldn't be in this mess if you would've just kept your legs together."

"What are you talking about?"

The two women began walking.

"You know damn well what I'm talking about. You sleeping with Toth, Gear, and Billy."

Candy stops short. "What? I told you earlier, I've never had sex with neither Gear nor Toth. You've got to be kidding me, right?" Candy brushes her reddening, dripping nose. "Is that what this is all about? You killed those men because you thought I slept with them?" Candy is sick to her stomach. Is this all her fault?

"I didn't kill them, you did. After you had sex with them." Cynthia screams at the top of her lungs.

"I didn't murder them, Cynthia." A boxed in silence surrounds them. No birds, wind, social noises, invade their space. "I swear."

"Then who did?"

"Oh, my gosh, Cynthia. You've got to let me go, we need to find the sheriff."

"Shut up! You're not going anywhere. People are going to think that I'm *Fruit Loops the Serial Killer*, me and only me." She pulls the gun out of her pocket and fires at Candy Jane, barely missing her. "I'm sick of you."

Seeing Cynthia take aim a second time, Candy runs. Her feet slipping out from beneath her, she falls just in time as the gunshot whizzes above her. Cynthia stumbles up behind her.

"Get up!" Her voice barking like a rabid Pit Bull.

Candy lay motionless for a moment, and then figuring her options are exhausted, she starts to get up, when suddenly Cynthia slips a noose around her neck and tightens it as Candy rises.

"Just try to get away, again." Cynthia tugs the rope. "Now, come on, your destiny awaits."

Candy's scared shitless. If Sheriff Anderson doesn't arrive soon, her fate is doomed, her goose cooked. Tears roll down her face, as Candy begins to pray. She only knows one prayer, the Hail Mary, but it's verse comforts her as they scurry down the pathway.

Jimmy squeezes Sheriff Anderson's mid-section. "Did you hear that?" He hugs him even tighter when he hears the second shot.

"Yes, Jimmy, I heard the shots, now let's go." Jon tries to loosen Jimmy's grip with his hand.

"We need to hurry, Cynthia might have killed her by now, and it will all be my fault."

"And why is it *your* fault?"

"I should have been more of a man and stood up for myself."

"Don't start that now, Jimmy. This isn't the time" Jon is beginning to believe that he made a mistake in bringing Jimmy along.

Coming upon Jimmy's car stuck in a snow drift, Jon sneaks up to it and touches the hood. "It's still warm, which means they couldn't have gotten far." He turns off the snow mobile, and dismounts.

Glancing down, he notices a few Fruit Loops scattered on the ground and then a slight path leading north. "Jimmy, you stay here and wait for Deputy Pickens. When he arrives, point him in the direction I'm going. Tell him to be quiet though, and wait for my signal."

"But, I want to go with you."

"No, Jimmy. I don't want you getting in the way."

"But I won't." Tugging at Jon's arm like a six year old.

"I said, no." Jon's voice is firm as he starts to follow the trail.

Creeping along, Jon suddenly thinks of the last time he and Carol had dinner at Sven's. They sat in the bar and he was watching the game on the TV over her shoulder while she went on about how nice Patricia always dressed and how much Carol liked a piece of jewelry the Swiss was wearing.

"The broche." Jon gasps. "It's not Cynthia's, but Patricia's. He's been after the wrong suspect."

Hearing Cynthia's muffled voice in the distance, Jon inches along the narrow path, hoping not to make a sound.

❈　❈　❈

"Come on, hurry up." Cynthia yanks on the rope. If she continues to tighten the noose, there'll be no need to toss her over the bridge, Candy thinks.

"I'm going as fast as I can. These boots aren't worth shit." Candy glances down at the Sorrels; it's time for a new pair.

Hearing something crack behind them, Candy doesn't react, not wanting to get Cynthia's attention. But she must have heard it too, because she turns and looks back.

"Did you hear anything?" She barks at Candy.

"Nope, just the wind." Candy prays it's Sheriff Anderson. He's becoming kind of like her knight in shining armor. She's always thought he's cute, but knowing he's been married forever, figures there's no chance. Candy has always just admired him from a distance. Shaking her head, she can't believe she's fantasying about romance at a time like this.

She's about to die!

They approach the bridge sooner than Candy expects. It's never been this close any other time she's been up here. Did they move it?

Cynthia stops and stomping toward her, pushes her back into a snow pile. Falling, Candy lands in a pillow of white. Removing the gun from her pocket, she warns. "You make a move and I'll shoot you, I won't kill you, just injure you so you'll feel pain during your last minutes on earth."

Candy doesn't know what suddenly comes over her, but she's tired of this, and surprisingly mouths back, not caring what happens. "Quit being so dramatic. It's really getting old."

Cynthia fires a shot at Candy, and misses. Sheriff Anderson, squatting sixty feet away, feels the whiz of the bullet against his check, and listens as the slug hits an Oak with a thug. He glances up to the sky, and makes the sign of the cross.

"That's it. How dare you talk to me like that. You're a no one. A nobody, my dog's craps have more worth than you."

"That's not a very nice thing to say." Candy razzes her assailant.

Rushing toward her, Cynthia slaps the tape across Candy's mouth. "Now, maybe you'll shut up."

Candy gathers by now that the noise from earlier is just the wind. All of her hopes vanish like wrinkles on a Botoxed aging actress. Panicking sweat dots Candy's skin and she starts to shiver.

Bending over, Cynthia helps Candy Jane up. For a brief instant, she lets go of the rope, and realizing this, Candy kicks Cynthia in the groin, and tries to run for it. She doesn't get very far, as Cynthia grabs the line and yanks it back.

Candy loses her breath as she falls to the ice. Cynthia lumbers toward her. "You stupid, stupid, bitch." She kicks Candy in the side. This time something breaks.

Breathing becomes hard for Candy as the duct tape keeps her from opening her mouth. She starts to gag, and Cynthia rips the adhesive from her lips.

"I can't breathe." Candy gasps. "I think you broke a rib."

"That's not my problem." Rolling Candy over to the edge of the bridge, the fated woman tries to desperately plead her case.

"Cynthia, please, don't do this. There has to be a better way. I've never done anything to you. You're mistaken.."

"You stole the love of my life."

"I told you, I didn't have anything to do with them."

"Liar!" She screams.

The day dips into a dark night, as Candy surrenders. There is no one coming to her rescue, and the pain in her chest continues to increase. She's going to die alone by the hands of this lunatic, for something she never did. Closing her eyes, she wishes Cynthia will just get it over with.

❋   ❋   ❋

"Hold it right there, Cynthia." A booming voice roars over the quiet.

Both women turn to see Patricia standing on the other side of the bridge holding a rifle.

"Let Candy Jane go!"

"This is none of your business, you foreign carpetbag-ger." Cynthia raises her gun and aims at Patricia."

"This is between you and me, and the lives you've ruined by being such a whore."

Cynthia edges away from Candy Jane, Sheriff Anderson waits in the brush, wondering who's gonna confess first.

"I have no idea what you're talking about."

Patricia inches closer to the two women. "You have no scruples, Cynthia, you'll screw any man no matter if he's involved with someone else or not."

"Hey, I didn't force any of those guys to have sex with me, they were all willing and able, if you get my drift." A light suddenly goes off in Cynthia's mind. "You killed them, you're the real *Fruit Loops the Serial Killer*. But why?"

"Because of you Cynthia. They were all tainted by your stench, and I had to execute them before they spread you nastiness to other women."

"Why you lousy bitch." Cynthia rushes at Patricia, and the two begin to wrestle on the icy bridge.

❋　❋　❋

Jon feels gutless as he rushes out from behind the snow bush, revolver in hand, screaming at the top of his lungs. "Okay, ladies, that's enough, stop it right now." But his words go unheard, as they struggle against the slick railing. As Patricia tries to push Cynthia, her feet tangle in the rope, and slipping, they both tumble over the icy barrier, screaming in unison as they plunge to their death.

Staggering toward Candy Jane who sits weeping on the frozen bridge, Jon looks over and sees the two bodies sprawled in a pool of blood on the white frozen river. Squatting down he removes the noose from her neck, and taking Candy in his arms, tries to comfort the distraught woman. He feels something familiar, but can't pin-point the sensation. Maybe it's just relief over the case finally being solved.

"Everything is alright now, Candy, neither of them can hurt you anymore."

Sniffling, and wiping her nose on her sleeve, Candy murmurs. "So it was Patricia all along. She's the one who killed those three men. But why?"

"I suppose she was jealous, that's what it sounded like to me. I heard the whole conversation."

"Why didn't you stop the fight."

"I wanted to hear a confession from one of them, and I

did. How would I know they'd both fall over the rail?" Jon lifts Candy to her feet, who staggers at first. "Come on let's get back to the snowmobile."

Jimmy can't take it anymore. He has to know what's going on. So, against Sheriff Anderson's orders, he slowly sneaks along the path. He sees two figures coming toward them, and realizing its Candy and the sheriff, runs to them as fast as the piled snow path will allow him. Falling to the ground, Jimmy grinds his chin into the ice, scraping a layer of skin off.

Watching, Jon and Candy begin to laugh, as Jimmy swipes the crystals off his clothes.

"Real sensitive the two of you are." Jimmy wraps his arms around Candy and starts to whimper. "I thought for sure you were a goner, what happened back there?"

"Well, it wasn't Cynthia at all, but Patricia. I guess she had a crush on Toth and witnessed Cynthia's prowess when it came to men, and went over the edge. I mean literally over the edge." Jon finishes.

The wailing sirens echo in the stillness of the darkening night, as Candy Jane stands on her tip-toes and kisses Jon on the cheek. The sheriff's arm is still around her waist, as she glances up into his eyes and sees a sparkle in them that makes her feel safe.

All in all, Candy Jane thinks, this is turning out to be the best day of her life.

ABOUT THE AUTHOR

Mary Maurice wrote her first poem when she was in the ninth grade, and hasn't stopped writing since. Catching the fire at an early age, she continues to dedicate her time to the craft.

Ms. Maurice has completed several novels of fiction and poetry, and has performed readings in distinct cities around the country. She presently resides in Santa Fe, New Mexico.

CPSIA information can be obtained
at www.ICGtesting.com
Printed in the USA
FSOW01n2334270816
24260FS